THE HAUNTED VALENTINE

A LIN COFFIN COZY MYSTERY BOOK 7

J. A. WHITING

J. A. WHITING BOOKS

To hear about new books and book sales, please sign up for my mailing list at:

www.jawhitingbooks.com

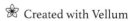 Created with Vellum

For my family with love

1

The summer sunlight filtered through the puffy white clouds sending a few shadows over the walkway where Lin Coffin and her cousin, Viv, strolled past the boats and yachts moored along the docks of Nantucket town. The young women had treated themselves to lunch in a restaurant that overlooked the water and they sat outside on the deck under an umbrella with the sea breeze gently pushing away the humidity as they enjoyed their sandwiches, salads, and French fries. A gull cawed overhead and the water lapped against the pier's pilings.

"I haven't been to the gift shop in ages," Viv said. "I'm looking for a pretty picture of a sailing boat.

Something small that would look nice over my desk in the living room. Not too expensive. Beth came into the bookstore yesterday and told me she'd just gotten in some things that I might like." Viv, who'd lived on the island almost all of her life, owned a bookstore-café on the main street of town and played in a band some nights each week with her Realtor boyfriend, John.

"I saw some nice drink coasters in her window when I walked by recently. They have different kinds of shells painted on them. I might buy them." Lin had her long brown hair pulled up in a ponytail and wore a summer skirt and a tank top that showed off the definition in her upper arms that she'd gained by working as a landscaper over the past year. Returning to the island of her birth from Cambridge, Massachusetts, Lin had bought the small business and after a few months, had joined forces with Leonard Reed, an experienced land-scaper, who she'd mistakenly thought was a murderer when they first met. Together they'd expanded their customer base and taken on bigger projects during their fruitful partnership.

Viv slipped her arm through Lin's. "I have an idea. Our birthday is coming up. Why don't you pick something out in the gift shop and I'll buy it as your birthday present and I'll choose something and you buy it for me." Lin and Viv shared the same birth date and would be turning thirty in a couple of weeks.

Lin eyed her cousin. "Why do I suspect an uneven exchange? The coasters I want aren't exactly equivalent in price to the painting you're interested in."

Viv chuckled and mischief danced in her eyes. "It's the thought behind the gift that counts, isn't it? Not the price."

With a smile, Lin shook her head as they walked along the brick sidewalk and crossed the cobble-stoned main street to the small road that led to the gift shop.

"I can't wait to have a look at this painting," Viv said entering the store and holding the door for Lin.

The beautiful gift shop had a crystal chandelier sparkling from the high ceiling, creamy mocha walls, and white shelves and tables holding jewelry, linens, candles, handmade Nantucket baskets, paintings, old maps, soft woven blankets, and other lovely household items. Viv called hello to Beth, the owner of the shop, and they walked to the back of the store where the painting of the sail boats hung on the wall.

As Lin moved from table to table looking for the coasters she was interested in, an odd feeling of apprehension washed over her and she shook herself trying to throw it off. She approached a white rectangular table covered with a pale blue linen cloth to see an artfully displayed collection of sailor's valentines.

Most valentines, a kind of shell craft, were octagonal in shape with a glass front hinged wooden box that displayed thousands of small sea shells of different colors laid out in intricate, symmetrical designs. Common designs included compass roses, hearts, a person's name, a loving message, flowers, an anchor, or other sea-related objects. The early valentines were made in the 1800s, many on the island of Barbados where sailors would purchase the beautiful shellwork to bring home to a family member or loved-one.

Lin's eyes wandered over the amazing designs and when she picked up one of them to get a closer look, her hand felt like it was lifting a block of ice. So surprised by the sensation, Lin fumbled with the valentine, but caught it with her other hand before it slipped completely from her grasp. She quickly set the wooden box back on the display table and started to move away, but something about the object made her turn back.

Lin leaned closer to the box and admired the tiny pinkish, cream, white, and purple shells formed into a repeating design of small and large flowers surrounding a cameo set in the middle of the box ringed by pink and white shells. The little shells formed the pattern of flowers that spread out from the cameo to the edges of the box. Thinking she had never seen anything so intricately beautiful, a sudden flood of emotions roiled through Lin's body ... love and friendship, hope, uncertainty, fear ... and a terrible, suffocating grief that nearly broke her heart. With her eyes filling with tears, Lin took several hurried steps away from the table as a whoosh of freezing air swirled around her.

"Lin," Viv called from the rear of the shop. "Come see this painting."

Lin sucked in a deep breath and forced her shaky legs to propel her to her cousin's side.

"Look at this." Viv stared at a twelve by fourteen-inch oil painting of a sailing ship moving through the ocean waves. "Look at the colors. Look at the water and the sails. It's like I'm right there watching the boat glide over the waves," Viv gushed.

When Lin didn't respond, Viv tore her eyes from the artwork and turned to her cousin. Seeing the odd look on Lin's face, she asked softly, "What's wrong with you?"

"Nothing," Lin said dully. Although she tried to focus on the picture of the sailboat, her mind kept wandering back to the sailor's valentine she'd seen at the front of the store.

Viv, the golden streaks in her light brown hair glimmering under the shop lights, stepped closer to Lin. "I know that look," she whispered. "What's going on?"

"Um," Lin mumbled. "I found those coasters I like."

Viv's blue eyes narrowed. "Did you see a ghost?"

Ever since she was little, Lin had the ability to see ghosts, but as a young girl, she'd decided she didn't want to experience any more visitations and the ghosts stopped making appearances. On her return to the island, however, spirits began to come to Lin for help and it didn't matter if she wanted to see them or not. When they needed something, they showed up.

"No." Lin shook her head. "I didn't see anything. Everything's okay."

Viv was undeterred. She put her hand on her hip. "No, everything isn't okay. Tell me what's going on."

Lin looked back over her shoulder. "I felt a little funny."

"When? What were you doing?"

"I was looking at the sailor's valentines." Lin gestured to the front of the store. "They're set up on the display table. Did you see them?"

"No. Show me." Viv gave her cousin an encouraging nod and they headed to the table with the arrangement of valentines.

When Viv saw the beautiful artwork made of shells, she leaned down to admire them. "Wow, these are some of the best I've ever seen. They must be antiques."

Beth, the shop owner, walked by. "Aren't they gorgeous? They're all from the 1800s. The work is amazing, isn't it?"

When Beth moved away, Viv looked at Lin. "Did you touch one of these? Were you attracted to one in particular?"

Lin hesitated, and then pointed. "I thought this one was especially pretty."

"You picked it up?" Viv was like an inquisitor.

Lin gave a little nod.

"And...?" Viv asked.

"It felt cold, really cold." Lin absent-mindedly rubbed her horseshoe necklace, an heirloom once owned by an ancestor, between her thumb and index finger.

Viv's eyes widened and her hand flew to the side of her face. "Cold?" She glanced around the shop looking for ghosts even though she'd never been able to see one in her life. "Is there ... *someone* in here?"

"I only felt the cold. I didn't see anyone."

A look of relief washed over Viv's rosy cheeks and she exhaled. "Okay. It might be nothing. Maybe you picked up some vibe about the person from long ago who made the valentine ... or maybe you sensed the person who bought it and carried it back to Nantucket." Viv took her cousin's arm. "I'm going to buy the ship picture. Let's go do that, and then let's get the heck out of here as fast as we can."

Lin stayed by Viv's side as Beth removed the painting from the wall, carefully bundled it in brown paper and bubble wrap, and rang up the sale. Something kept tugging at Lin and every few seconds, she looked back to the table of valentines.

"All set." Viv held her prize in her hand and headed for the door looking anxious and eager to exit the shop. "We can leave now."

Reaching for the doorknob, Viv paused when her cousin said, "I didn't get the coasters."

Viv forced a smile. "Why don't we do that another day? We should be heading home."

"I'd like to get them." Lin turned around. Once again, her senses flooded with the emotions she'd felt when gazing at the valentine and a wall of icy air enveloped her as she walked past the display table and paused. "I wonder how much this is." Lin gestured to the shellwork encased in the lovely wooden box.

Viv hurried over and tugged on Lin's arm. "I bet its way too expensive. These are antiques. We can't afford them."

Beth came to the table, lifted the valentine that Lin had shown interest in, and checked the tag.

When she heard the price, Lin winced.

"See. Too expensive." Viv put her hand on her cousin's arm to steer her to the door. "You have great taste, but not a budget to match."

Feeling almost dizzy, Lin stared at the tiny pink, purple, and white shells and she reached her hand out to touch the antique box. When her fingers set against the polished wood, it was as if she was touching dry ice ... the valentine almost burned her skin.

Raising her eyes to the store owner, Lin's words caused Viv to let out a little groan. With a voice barely above a whisper, Lin told the woman, "I'll take it."

2

———

"My fingers don't burn any more when I hold the valentine." Lin placed her new purchase on the sideboard hutch in the kitchen and stepped back to admire it.

"Thank the heavens for little favors," Viv said looking at the object with suspicion. "Why would it burn you? Why would burning someone's skin make a person want to buy the thing?"

When the cousins returned to the house, Lin's little brown dog, Nicky, and Viv's gray cat, Queenie, woke from their nap in the bedroom and walked sleepy-eyed into the kitchen. Nicky greeted Lin and Viv and then stood up on his hind legs, trying to sniff the air around the valentine.

Queenie glanced at the young women and

jumped onto a stool at the kitchen island where she sat and turned her attention to Lin's purchase. The cat's eyes were glued to the valentine and her tail swished rhythmically back and forth.

"These two sure are interested in that thing." Viv took another look at the shellwork and then went to the refrigerator for the pitcher of iced tea.

"It's really beautiful, isn't it?" Lin cocked her head while gazing at the object.

Viv poured the tea over ice cubes in two tall glasses. "Yes, especially when it isn't burning your skin when you touch it."

With a chuckle, Lin sat next to her cousin and lifted one of the glasses to her lips. "As soon as I saw it, I was drawn to it. I had to buy it. I couldn't leave it at the store."

Viv knew all about her cousin's ability to see ghosts and she'd been pulled into helping solve several mysteries on the island since Lin had returned to make Nantucket her permanent home. Viv and Lin were descended from some of the island's earliest settlers and some of those ancestors had paranormal powers. Those powers had been passed down to Lin from both her mother's *and* father's sides.

Once as a young girl, Lin made the mistake of

confiding the news of her skills to someone she thought was a friend only to have the child spread the information throughout their entire school until Lin was mercilessly teased and shunned. Lin and her grandfather left that town shortly after the incident and moved to Cambridge where Lin figured out how to keep ghosts from appearing to her.

Viv turned her head for a moment to have another look at the valentine. "Why do you think you were drawn to it?"

"I don't know." Lin shrugged a shoulder.

"It's going to pull us into something, isn't it?" Viv crossed her arms over her chest in a defensive posture. "It's haunted, isn't it?"

"We don't know that." Although she said the words, Lin didn't really believe her hopeful comment. "It might just be what you said at the store. I might just be sensing the person who made it, or the person who bought it, or owned it." She gave her cousin a smile.

"Or," Viv's eyes narrowed, "it's going to draw us into something."

Lin put her chin in her hand. "Maybe."

"What do you know about these sailor's valentines?" Viv asked.

"A lot of them came from Barbados and were

bought by sailors who had been on long sailing journeys and wanted to take a souvenir back home to a loved one. I've read that many of the valentines were made by the women of Barbados."

"So are you sensing the woman who made it?"

"I don't know who it is." Lin got up, went to the sideboard, and brought the valentine to the kitchen island. She ran her hand over the glass front and along the wooden sides while staring at the intricate patterns of the tiny shells. Lin's hand became warm, but her skin didn't feel like she was touching a hot coal like she'd experienced while in the gift shop.

The kitchen opened to a wide deck that ran between the sides of the horseshoe- shaped house and something seemed to move outside beyond the screen door. Lin looked up and Nicky let out a woof, but whatever was out there was gone. A bird maybe, or a squirrel Lin thought.

"I'm starting that new landscaping job tomorrow." Heading to the fridge to get the pistachio gelato pie she'd made, Lin carried it to the kitchen island and sliced pieces for Viv and herself. She needed to talk about something besides the valentine. Even though she felt compelled to buy the item, the unknown aspects of the thing were unnerving her.

"That's Jeff's friend's place?" Viv took a forkful of the pie and closed her eyes. "Delicious. So light and refreshing. I should put this on the menu at the bookstore."

Lin thanked her cousin for the compliment. "Jeff's friend, Neil, owns an antique Cape house off of the Polpis Road. Neil's going away for a month on business and while he's gone, we'll re-landscape his property."

"Will Neil being away make the project more difficult?" Viv asked.

"We've gone over everything with him. If something comes up, then I'll email and send pictures. It will work out fine."

"Jeff is working on the house?"

Lin gave a nod as she swallowed some of the gelato pie. "He's doing some renovation work for Neil. It will take about three weeks for Jeff to finish everything."

"Is Leonard going to work with you on the project?" Viv asked as she wiped her lips with a napkin and eyed the pie pondering whether or not she should have another piece.

"Leonard will work there most of the time. We have a lot of work at the moment so he'll be handling other things while we do Neil's place." Lin smiled and flexed her arm to make a little muscle. "I've gotten in great shape doing all of this heavy outside work."

"I don't know how you do it. I couldn't handle doing landscaping no matter how trim it would make me." Viv shook her head. "I can't work in the heat. Give me the air-conditioned bookstore any day. I have no idea how Leonard works so hard, at his age, in the heat and humidity. It would kill me."

"Leonard's only in his early sixties. He's in better shape than both of us." Lin chuckled. "And it's a good thing he didn't hear that comment of yours. He isn't old."

Viv waved away Lin's reprimand. "You know what I mean."

Lin's phone beeped with a text. "Speak of the devil. It's Leonard. He's asking if I can pick him up in the morning." She sent a return text and set the phone down. "You know, it's kind of weird. Leonard has never once invited me into his house."

"Why is that weird?" Viv asked.

"Well, isn't it?" Lin made eye contact with her cousin. "Leonard's been here in my house a million times, he's eaten with us, he even slept on the sofa one night to protect me when we were involved in that other case. He's been to your house a bunch of times, too, but he's never once invited me into his house."

"Maybe the place is a mess. Maybe he doesn't want you to see what a messy person he is."

"When I first met him, I would have thought that was the reason, but not now." Lin moved her fork over her plate to pick up the last of the pie crumbs. "I should drive you past his house one day. It's a small, antique Cape, perfectly tended. There's a white picket fence around the front yard. It's filled with flowers and flowering bushes, and I mean *filled*. It's like something out of a magazine. It's gorgeous. And you should see how neat and tidy the outside of the house is. We should use his place as a testimonial to his landscaping abilities. It's that perfect." Lin sipped her iced tea. "I'm sure the inside is done just as nicely."

Viv got an idea. "Ask him about the history of his house, then maybe he'll ask you in to see it."

"I did that. He answered my questions and that was it."

Viv gave a chuckle. "Maybe he's got a dead body hidden in there."

Nicky and Queenie sat side by side looking out to the deck through the kitchen's screen door. The dog turned his head and barked at Viv.

Viv's comment caused a shiver to run over Lin's skin and a serious expression to form on her face.

Viv noticed Lin's reaction. "I'm kidding, for Pete's sake." She looked over at Nicky and said to the dog, "You know Leonard. He doesn't have a dead body in his house." Viv narrowed her eyes and used a sinister-sounding voice to kid them. "Or does he?"

Lin let out a groan. "I guess I'll just have to keep wondering why Leonard won't let me inside his house."

Viv stood up to load the dishwasher with the dirty plates and glasses. "It was nice to have the afternoon off with you, but I'd better go check on the bookstore and make sure everything's okay."

Lin let the dog and cat outside and then went to cover the pie with plastic wrap. Movement at the living room window caught her eye and she craned her neck to see a man heading for her front landing. He walked briskly and was wearing a long-sleeved shirt and brown slacks. "There's someone coming to the door."

"Is there? I'll go see." Viv walked through the living room and opened the door. She stepped out and then came right back in. "There's no one here. Maybe the person walked past the house."

Lin shook her head. "No. He was on my walkway. He was definitely coming to this house."

"Well, there's no one out there." Viv came back to the kitchen and then stopped suddenly and stared at her cousin. "Are you cold?" Lin always felt cold whenever a ghost was around.

"No, I'm not cold. I saw the man through the window." Lin gestured.

"Maybe he realized he had the wrong address," Viv suggested.

"And what? Evaporated? He couldn't have gotten very far. He must have been on the street when you looked out."

Viv leveled her eyes at Lin. "I looked up and down the road. There wasn't anyone nearby. Unless he stepped into the trees to hide."

Lin had a dumbfounded look on her face. "He looked like he was in his early twenties, he was medium height, thin. He had a beard. It was dark brown like his hair. He was dressed in slacks and a matching vest and a white shirt...." She stopped talking and her mouth hung open a little as she blinked. "Did I imagine him?"

Was he out there or not?

3

The early morning sun peeked through the trees as Lin parked her truck at the end of Leonard's driveway, let the dog out of the vehicle, and headed to the door to ring the bell. Before she could press the button, the tall, strong man came around from the back of the house carrying his lunch box in one hand and his tool case in the other. He set the tool box down to pat the dog as it danced around his legs. Nicky practically grinned as Leonard scratched behind the dog's ears.

"Mornin', Coffin," he said to Lin with a nod. "I'm all ready to go."

Wanting to see how Leonard responded to her request, Lin asked, "Can I use your bathroom?"

"The house is a mess. I don't let anyone in when

it looks like that." Leonard opened the truck's passenger side door. "Go around back and pee in the woods."

Lin gave the man a frown. "Thanks, but no thanks. I'll wait until we get to the work site." Ideas about why Leonard wouldn't let her inside his home swirled around in her mind, but none of them seemed to be plausible. She didn't believe the reason he gave her that the house was too messy ... the place couldn't be that big of a mess. Climbing into the driver's side, Lin eyed her business partner wondering what the real reason was for keeping her out of his home.

When they arrived at the site of the new project, Lin's boyfriend, Jeff, had already arrived and was removing some tools from the bed of his truck. He heard Lin pulling into the crushed shell driveway and gave her and Leonard a wide smile and a wave.

"I just got here." Jeff greeted them.

Lin gave the handsome carpenter a hug and a kiss and Nicky rubbed his head against Jeff's leg until the man gave the little dog some pats. In his mid-thirties, tall and fit with dark brown hair and brown eyes, Jeff had been an Air Force pilot for eight years before returning to the island of his birth to work as a self-employed carpenter.

The three people and the dog headed to the backyard, a half-acre of weedy grass with shade trees standing along the rear of the property line. A long row of blooming blue hydrangeas grew to the left and right sides of the place. A similar antique Cape-style house stood on the lot to the right and a rambling old Colonial was on the left.

"It's a nice yard," Jeff remarked. "It has lots of possibilities. My buddy is looking forward to the transformation." Looking over to the beautiful flowering bushes, he asked, "Does Neil want to keep the hydrangeas?"

"He does," Lin told him with a nod.

"Good. They're too beautiful to get rid of and they're sort of a Nantucket tradition."

"If Neil asked for us to pull them out," Lin said with a grin, "Leonard and I would have tried to talk him out of it. We would have encouraged him to keep them."

"Most of the time, we can be pretty persuasive." With Nicky trotting after him, Leonard headed over to the pile of tools they'd dropped off previously and took hold of one of the wheelbarrows.

Lin described the landscaping plans to Jeff. "We're putting in flower beds along these sides, a stone patio is going right off the kitchen door with a path to that part of the yard over there where we'll build a stone base for the gazebo Neil has ordered. There will be an arbor on the other side," Lin gestured, "that will lead to a secret garden with a water feature and several benches."

"Sounds great." Jeff gave a nod of approval. He and Lin went into Neil's house so that Jeff could show his girlfriend the work he was doing. After the tour, Lin went back outside, marked out where one of the beds would go and got to work removing the lawn with a shovel. After an hour of working and swigging from a water bottle, Leonard came over to where Lin had cut the new bed.

"Taking a break to supervise me?" Lin kidded the man as she wiped beads of sweat from her forehead.

"Sometimes you need supervising," Leonard joked. "Listen, Coffin, I just got a text from Mrs. Lucien. She's having a fit over some of the flowers we put in her yard. She's hosting some kind of an afternoon tea thing for her friends in a few hours and she wants us to replace the flowers."

Lin rolled her eyes. Mrs. Lucien was a perfectionist who demanded everything look tip-top, even when it already did. "What's wrong with the flowers? I put them in two days ago."

"She changed her mind about the colors of the

flowers," Leonard went on to explain. "She thought the pink and white would look great with her table-cloths or whatever, but now she's changed her mind. She's in a panic. She wants them changed to add some blue in between." Leonard shrugged. "The customer is always right."

"Want me to go?" Lin leaned on the handle of the shovel.

"Nah, I'll do it. My winning personality will calm her down." Leonard downed the last of the water in his bottle. "I'll go by the greenhouse and pick out some things to make her happy." Lin and Leonard had begun renting some space from a big nursery on the island in order to have a wide supply and different assortment of flowers and bushes available when they needed them. "I'll need to borrow your truck."

Lin fished the keys out of her back pocket and handed them to her partner.

"I'll be back as soon as I finish up with Mrs. Lucien." Leonard headed for the truck.

Lifting her arms over her head and moving from side to side to stretch her back, Lin looked across the yard to see her dog resting on the grass in the shade of some trees. Deciding she needed a break, she took her water and a bowl from her cooler bag and went to join Nicky under the tree where the air felt ten degrees cooler in the shade.

She poured some water into the bowl for the dog and resting back against the tree trunk, Lin took a long swallow from the bottle thinking about Viv's comment that there was no way she'd ever work outside in the heat. Sometimes, Lin thought her cousin had a good point.

A rustling sound behind her caused Lin to swivel around on her butt. A man was working in the next yard pulling out some weeds from a flower bed that ran along the property line shared with Neil's place.

Lin called out a greeting and the man looked over at her.

"Hello. I didn't see you there." The man was in his late-twenties, slim, with dark brown hair and a short beard. He stood up and brushed at the knees of his chinos.

Lin walked over and introduced herself. "My partner and I are landscaping Neil's yard." Looking over to the antique gray-shingled Cape, she said, "Your house is lovely."

"Oh, it isn't my house. I'm the caretaker. I manage a few houses on this road and several others in town." The young man glanced at the Cape house. "I'd love to own a house like this someday."

He turned and smiled at Lin. "I'm saving my money."

"How long have you lived on the island?" she asked.

"My whole life." The man got a faraway look on his face. "It was a wonderful place to grow up."

"I was born here, too, but moved away when I was little," Lin said. "My grandfather raised me."

"Your parents died." The man said it in a factual way, not as a question.

"Yes, in an automobile accident."

"I'm very sorry. I've suffered loss, too."

Lin waited to hear some details, but the man glanced over to the house for a few moments without adding more information to his comment and she decided not to ask about his loss, thinking if he wanted to tell her, he would have. Such a strong sense of sadness floated around the man that the heaviness of it pressed against Lin's chest.

In contrast to Lin's impression, the young man turned back to Lin with a smile. "I got married recently."

Lin returned the smile. "Congratulations."

The man noticed Lin's necklace. "That's a beautiful necklace you're wearing."

Instinctively, Lin's hand moved to touch her

horseshoe necklace and before she could say anything, the man remarked, "It's an heirloom, isn't it?"

"It is. It belonged to a long-ago ancestor of mine."

The man stared tenderly at Lin's piece of jewelry. "I'd bet you are very much like her."

Surprised at the comment, Lin's eyebrow raised and then she said, "I think I am." The delicate horseshoe necklace had once belonged to Emily Witchard Coffin, who was one of the early settlers of the island, wife of Sebastien Coffin, and a relative of Lin's. Many of the Witchard women had "special" skills and Emily was no exception. It was believed that the woman could see ghosts, just like Lin was able to do.

"What was your relative's name?" the man asked.

Lin told him.

His soft, kind eyes rested on the necklace again. "Yes," he said, so softly that Lin barely heard the word. Not knowing why, a shiver danced over her skin.

Lin gave herself a shake. "Do you live nearby?"

"Not far. You live in town, isn't that right?"

"Just at the edge of town. How did you know?"

"I might have seen your truck around." The man

glanced over his shoulder back to the Cape. "I should get back to work. I'm pleased to make your acquaintance, Lin Coffin."

Lin was about to extend her hand to shake with him, but the man reached down for his weeding tool and turned around to walk back to the house so she and Nicky went back to Neil's yard. As she looked over the hydrangea bushes into the other house's yard, Lin couldn't see the man anywhere around the house he was tending.

Bending to pick up her shovel, a light cool breeze brushed over her skin and she realized the man hadn't told her his name.

Nicky woofed and Lin jumped. "You startled me, Nick," she told the dog with a chuckle. "What are you woofing about? You want me to get back to work? Did Leonard tell you to keep an eye on me?" She patted the dog's head and picked up her shovel. "Come on, let's get back to making that new flower bed."

Lin took one more look into the neighbor's yard and the thought that the man hadn't told her his name picked at her again. Why didn't he?

Lin's eyes widened. *He said my full name. I don't remember telling him my last name.*

4

As soon as Viv was free, she came over to the table Lin was sitting at in the bookstore. Queenie and Nicky rested in an upholstered chair near one of the long book shelves.

"This is the first minute I've had all day. It's been go, go, go since I opened the doors this morning. Someone called out sick and customers have been coming in droves."

Lin smiled as she broke off a piece of her corn muffin. "It's a good problem to have."

"Yes, but I'm not a marathon runner." Viv leaned back against her chair and yawned. Her face looked exhausted. "I need to build my stamina if we're going to have more days like this in the store. And tonight, John and I and the band are playing in a pub down by the docks. I'm going to fall asleep right in the middle of a song."

Lin chuckled. "I'll come just to see that happen."

"How was your first day on the new project?"

Lin's face clouded even though she responded positively. "We're off to a good start."

Viv narrowed her eyes. "But...?"

Lin let out a breath and told her cousin about the man who worked as a caretaker at the house next to Neil's. "It kind of unnerved me. The guy seemed to know things about me."

"Because he knew your last name?" Viv moved her hand dismissively. "You and Leonard are known around the island because of your business and your reputation for doing excellent work. Even people who have never met you might know who you are. You're out there doing landscaping work, your name is Lin ... people put two and two together and assume you're Carolin Coffin." Viv went on. "This man was a caretaker. He must have heard of you and Leonard. He figured out who you were."

"I don't know." Lin rested her hand in her chin. "There was more to it than that."

"What do you mean?" Viv questioned.

"He admired my necklace." Lin reached up and touched the horseshoe.

Vic cocked her head. "So? It's a beautiful necklace."

"He asked if it was an heirloom."

"Maybe the guy likes jewelry. Maybe he could tell it was an antique piece."

Lin blew out a breath and leaned forward. "He seemed to know that my parents died in an accident. He said I was probably a lot like the ancestor who had owned the necklace."

"Your last name is Coffin. If the man had lived here all of his life, he would know about the Coffin family." Viv shrugged a shoulder. "I think you're being too suspicious. What do you think he is? A stalker?"

Lin stared at her cousin pondering her words.

"Oh for heaven's sake, he couldn't be a stalker," Viv said, "he was working. You were working. He didn't follow you there."

"I don't think he's a stalker." Lin's face was serious.

"What *do* you think?"

"I don't know. The interaction felt weird. I don't know how to describe it."

Viv's eyes held her cousin's. "Did he make you feel cold?"

"No, he didn't make me feel cold. He *talked* to me

... with words. He's not a ghost." Even though Lin could see ghosts and sometimes sensed things from them, she'd never met a spirit who talked to her. Not once. "He talks ... so he isn't a ghost."

"Okay, good." Viv's expression was full of relief. "He's just some guy who's lived on the island forever, has heard of you and Leonard, and figured out you're Lin Coffin. That's all. No need to worry."

Something about the conversation with the care-taker still picked at Lin despite Viv's rational explanations.

Viv asked, "What about that valentine? Are you sensing anything from it? Has it started to burn your skin again when you touch it?"

"No, it's normal now. It's like a normal decorative piece that anyone might have on display in their house. I might have been reading too much into it."

Viv looked skeptical. "It wasn't burning you? You made that all up?"

Lin said, "When it was in the store, it felt like it was too hot to hold, but I could have been letting my mind run away with crazy ideas. I could have been picking up slight things about its origin and its prior owners and maybe I got too excited and exaggerated what I was feeling."

Viv crossed her arms over her chest. "Have you

ever done that before? Exaggerated a feeling you were having?"

"I ... I ... well, I might have."

"Can you come up with a specific example of a time you exaggerated a sensation?"

Lin thought for a few moments. "I can't think of one right off the bat."

"Neither can I, so I don't think you were exaggerating yesterday. You were feeling what you were feeling."

"Whatever I was picking up on has gone dim," Lin said. "The valentine seems normal."

"For now...." Viv warned. "Keep your eye on that thing. I don't think it's over. I think its resting ... or something."

A smile crept over Lin's mouth. "I'll take that under consideration."

"Don't smile at me like that," Viv scolded. "Once you start picking up on something, it never dissolves or evaporates or dissipates. No. This is only the beginning."

The smile on Lin's face disappeared. Her cousin was right. No matter how much she wanted to believe the valentine had settled because she'd purchased it, she knew, deep down, it wanted something from her.

Viv said with a sigh, "Time will tell what we're about to get dragged into."

Lin's face clouded with concern. "If you've had enough of ghosts and crimes and cases, I'll understand if you don't want to deal with any more of that stuff."

A longer line had formed at the café counter and Viv nodded to Mallory who was working alone preparing the coffee drinks and serving the desserts. Viv turned her gaze on her cousin. "If you think I'd let you have all the fun with the ghosts, you are sorely mistaken." Standing up to go help at the coffee bar, she said, "We need to plan our birthday party. We'll only turn thirty once so we better come up with something fun." Viv stood still and looked across the room at nothing. "Thirty. Yikes. Time sure does fly. We'll be old hags before we know it."

Lin smiled. "Hopefully, we have a few good years left before we become old hags."

"Are you sure it hasn't happened already?" a man's voice said. Anton Wilson, author, professor of history, and expert on all things Nantucket swept over to Lin's table and took the seat that Viv had been sitting in. In his sixties, quick and spry, Anton looked over his black-rimmed glasses with a smile on his face, pleased with his teasing of the young women.

"Are you calling us hags?" Viv asked with a hand on her hip.

"I only asked if you might have become such a thing already. You were the one who said that word, not me."

"I'll instruct everyone at the coffee bar not to wait on you." Viv left to go work behind the counter.

"Is she angry with me?" Anton leaned forward, worry etched over his brow.

"No, she's playing with you," Lin assured the man. "Don't worry, Viv can take a joke."

"That's a relief." Anton pulled a tattered book, some papers, a notebook, and his laptop from his briefcase. Without looking over at Lin, he said, "What's new with you?"

Anton was one of the few people who knew about Lin's "skill." She told him about the valentine.

Anton listened quietly and blinked at Lin before responding. He cleared his throat and said evenly, "That's very interesting."

Lin asked, "Do you have any theories about why I felt the heat coming off the valentine?"

"The piece was most likely created in the Caribbean. Perhaps you were sensing the hot days of the island's weather." Anton tapped the end of a pencil against his chin. "But that seems too simple. Maybe Libby and I should come by and take a look at it."

Libby Hartnett was an older woman who'd lived all of her life on the island and was a very distant relative of Lin's. Libby had special powers, too, and she'd helped Lin better understand and come to terms with her ability to see and interact with ghosts.

"I haven't seen Libby lately. Is she off-island?" Lin asked.

"She'll be back in a couple of days. I'll call you when we can come by."

Lin nodded and told Anton about her conversation with the caretaker who was working next door to Neil's house.

"I think Viv is probably right about the man. He's probably familiar with your landscaping company and knows a few things about you via the grapevine." Anton began clicking on the keys of his laptop.

Lin sipped the last of her tea and ate the final section of her corn muffin. She glanced over to see the dog and cat snoozing away in the chair and it made her fully aware of the fatigue she was feeling.

Unable to stifle a yawn, Lin wanted nothing more than to head home, shower, and take a nap on her comfy sofa before making a late dinner and then doing some programming work for the Cambridge company she worked for remotely on a part-time basis. Lin liked having the extra work so that when her landscaping jobs dried up in the winter she could supplement her income. She'd planned to see Viv and John play at the pub later that night, but she had to be up at the crack of dawn the next day and decided that staying in and hitting the sack early would be the wisest thing to do.

Lin also had the urge to go home to have another look at the valentine so she said goodbye to Anton, waved to Viv, roused the dog from his slumber, and headed out of the bookstore and up Main Street towards her cottage ... with a very strong sense of unease pulling at her.

5

Lin stood in the kitchen, her eyes traveling over every miniature shell and pattern line of the sailor's valentine. The soft, muted colors and the intricate details combined to create an incredible piece of artwork. Reaching out her hand, she picked up the valentine and carried it into the living room where she sank into the sofa's cushions. Nicky jumped up beside his owner, turned twice in a circle, and then settled against Lin's leg for a nap.

Lin leaned forward and brought the wooden box closer to her face so she could better see the shells. After a few minutes of inspection, she rested the valentine on her lap, ran her hand over the glass cover, and wondered about the person who made it, the person who bought it and carried it all the way to Nantucket, and about the fortunate person who received it as a gift.

In the 1800s, the majority of valentine buyers were sailors, men who had been away from home traveling on a ship often for at least a year's time. Far from their loved ones and the places they knew, the sailors made the unique purchase for that special someone who waited for their safe return.

Lin's eyelids became heavy and, try as she might, she couldn't keep them from slipping shut and as she dozed off, her head lolled back against the soft sofa.

Images flitted in her brain while she slept ... a ship heaving and falling on huge waves in a driving rainstorm, several men sitting on the deck under the stars sharing a smoke by passing around a single pipe of tobacco, the amazing blue of the Caribbean sea, the impossible green lushness of the island of Barbados, a sailor standing alone on a ship's deck with a single tear tracing down his cheek while staring at a small, crumpled-around-the-edges note of love from a shy, dark-haired young woman.

A loud *clunk* made Lin's eyes snap open and, at the same time, the dog startled, scrambled to his feet, and let out a woof. In the darkening room, Lin's and Nicky's heads spun from side to side looking for the source of the noise. With her heart pounding in her ears, Lin tried to figure out what had caused the sound. She slid to the edge of the sofa cushion and reached down to pat the dog. "Maybe a bird flew into the window?"

Nicky turned his head to look up at her as if to check whether or not he could relax or should stay on guard.

Lin stood and walked around the rooms with the dog padding after her, and not finding anything out of order, she wondered if she'd dreamt the noise and by jumping to consciousness, scared the dog. "Did you hear something, Nick, or did I startle you when I woke up so fast?"

The dog let out a whine causing Lin to smile. "Not sure, huh?" She ran her hand through her dark hair. "I don't see anything wrong or broken so it was either a noise from outside or I dreamt it."

Heading to the kitchen, she said, "Let's get our dinner. It's dark already. I need to do some programming work before I can crawl into bed." Lin would have loved to eat a bowl of cereal for dinner and then carry a cup of tea to her bedroom, slide under the covers, and work on crossword puzzles for an hour before turning out the light.

She fed the dog, made some spaghetti and a green salad, and defrosted a vegetable sauce that she ladled over the angel-hair pasta before sprinkling the dish with grated cheese. After eating and cleaning up, Lin headed for the spare bedroom that she used as an office, and within two hours, had completed the programming tasks that needed to be finished. With a yawn, she rubbed at her neck trying to loosen up the kinks that had gathered there and then answered some texts from Jeff and Leonard.

It was too late for puzzle books, so Lin shut off the kitchen lights and started for her bedroom. A shaft of moonlight came in through the window and lit up the valentine on the hutch like a spotlight was shining on it. Lin stopped and admired how lovely the shellwork looked in the light of the moon, and on impulse, lifted the wooden octagonal box and carried it into her room where she set it on her dresser.

Although the box of shells had stopped giving off heat, Lin felt such a strong pull from the creation that it almost made her uneasy. She tried to shake off the feeling by attempting to convince herself it was only because the artwork was so beautiful that she couldn't help staring at it.

Lin forced her eyes away from the box, climbed

44

into bed, turned off the bedside lamp, and shortly after her head hit the pillow, she was out like a light.

Clunk.

Lin woke with a start, but stayed perfectly still, listening. From the floor at the foot of her bed, the dog let out a low, heavy growl that rumbled in his throat. Lin wanted to shush him, but she kept silent. What was that noise? *Clunk.* The sound came from outside.

Lin slid out of bed and shuffled across the wood floor to the window where she pushed back the blinds an inch to peek out. Her forehead crinkled at what she saw.

Going to the front door and opening it a crack, she called to the man in the road. "Do you need help?"

Nicky stuck his head through the slight open door to get a look out front.

Under the streetlamp, a huge horse, almost as big as a Clydesdale, stood next to a man in his twenties who was wearing wool slacks, a white shirt with the sleeves rolled up, and a tweed cap. In his hand, he held a lead-line that was attached to the horse's halter.

"We're fine. Sorry to bother." The man touched his cap and lifted it a little as he nodded to Lin with a smile. "My horse's shoe is loose. My friend down the road," the man gestured, "knows something about blacksmithing, but he didn't have the right tools to fix it. We're heading home now. Sorry if we woke you."

"It's okay." Lin watched the man lead the horse forward, the huge animal making a clunking sound each time his right, rear foot hit the road. "Do you have far to go?"

"Not at all. A couple of miles. We'll be fine." He tipped his hat again, and whistling a tune, kept on up the road until Lin couldn't see them anymore.

Nicky and Lin exchanged glances.

Lin said, "Well, you don't see that outside your door every day, do you?" When she shut and locked the door, a cold shaft of air surrounded her and the dog whined and focused his attention into the living room.

Afraid to turn around, Lin hesitated, took in a long breath, and swiveled on her feet to look in the direction that Nicky was facing.

The room was empty.

Taking a few steps forward, Lin spoke softly, "Is anyone there?"

Sliding her feet to bring her closer to the wall, she

reached over and flicked the light switch to illuminate the living room. The sudden brightness made her eyes clamp shut for a few seconds. When she opened her lids, a quick movement of something flashed from the room into the kitchen leaving behind a wave of cold air that blew in Lin's direction. She darted for the kitchen and stopped short, her heart in her throat.

An old man stood near the far wall next to the window in the shaft of moonlight.

A ghost.

His thin hair was gray and his eyes looked watery and tired. He wore brown slacks and a brown overcoat and he held a hat in his hands. His shoulders were stooped.

In her thin sleep shorts and pajama tank top, Lin was almost shaking from the freezing air in the room. She wrapped her arms around herself. Nicky stood quietly at attention next to Lin's leg.

"Hello." Lin's voice was practically a whisper.

The old man made eye contact with her, but he didn't speak. They never did.

"Do you need help?" Lin asked.

The ghost just stared at her.

Lin asked softly, "Were you a sailor once?"

The man's shoulders hunched even more.

"Is the valentine yours?" Lin took one step forward.

The man blinked.

"I don't know how to help." Lin kept her eyes on the man. "I'm not sure what to do."

The old man gave such a slight nod it would have been easy to miss.

Lin touched her horseshoe necklace. "Did you give the valentine to someone on Nantucket? Did you give it to someone you loved?"

A single glistening tear spilled from the man's eye.

Lin's heart clenched at the sight. "I want to help," she said gently. "I want to figure out what you need."

The ghost's form began to shimmer and it slowly became more and more translucent. He was about to disappear.

Lin moved a step closer. "Don't go. Can you stay a little longer?"

The man blinked several times. His body had become so see-through that Lin knew he'd be gone in a moment.

The sadness pouring from the man made Lin's stomach tighten. "I'll figure it out. I won't give up," she told the ghost.

In a few seconds, Lin and her dog were alone in the room, the cold sucked out and away.

"I promise," Lin whispered to the empty space.

Her hand went to the side of her face and the urge to cry crashed over her. With a heart heavy and sorrowful, Lin looked down at her sweet dog. "Come on, Nick. Let's go back to bed."

Blinking back tears, she flicked off the kitchen light, turned, and saw something on the hutch.

The sailor's valentine was back on the shelf, the moonlight lighting it up in the darkness.

6

L in and Jeff stood by the grill adding hamburgers and veggie burgers to the already cooking baked potatoes and corn on the cob. Viv placed a pasta salad and a jug of homemade sangria on the deck table and then set out the plates and silverware.

Lin had just finished telling them about the first odd thing that happened the previous night. "A horse. Right outside on the street."

"Are you sure you didn't dream that?" Lighting the jar candles on the table, Viv looked at her cousin with skepticism.

"I'm sure. Nicky saw it, too." Lin glanced down at the dog resting on the patio lounge chair with Queenie. "Right, Nick?"

The dog put his nose in the air and barked in agreement.

"See?" Lin asked.

"If the dog says it's so, then I believe it," Jeff kidded.

Lin looked at Viv. "You don't believe I saw a horse in the street, but I bet you'll believe what I tell you happened next."

With a wary expression, Viv narrowed her eyes. "What happened next? The horse came in for tea?"

Lin ignored the comment. "A ghost paid a visit."

Jeff and Viv stared at Lin.

"What happened?" Viv asked cautiously.

Lin told them about her late night visitor. "He made me feel so sad. He broke my heart and I don't know over what. I told him I'd figure out what he needed." She bit her lower lip. "What if I can't do it?"

Jeff went to Lin's side and wrapped his arm over her shoulders. "You've been able to help the ghosts in the past. You'll be able to do it this time, too."

"I shouldn't have promised him." Lin pushed a stray strand of her hair from her eyes. "The day might come when I can't help. I don't want to disappoint him. He needs something. I have to figure it out."

Viv moved closer with an encouraging smile.

"One step at a time. That's how you always do it." She nodded at Jeff. "And we're here ... and Libby and Anton, too ... we'll all help. Even though we can't see the spirits, we can offer moral support and you can bounce ideas off of us."

A grin crept over Lin's mouth. "I'm grateful for your help, and you're right, one step at a time." Even though she truly appreciated her cousin's kind support, she always felt helpless and overwhelmed when a new ghost came to her, afraid she wouldn't be able to accomplish what they needed. She pushed down her worry and apprehension so that she could enjoy the evening with her friends. "Should we put the food in the oven to keep it warm?" Lin asked. "What time do you think John will get here?"

Viv's boyfriend had met a client to show a house and was running late. As if on cue, John came around the side of the house carrying a side dish of mozzarella squares topped with slices of fresh tomatoes drizzled with seasoned olive oil. "I had to stop by the boat to change and pick up the cheese and tomatoes. Everything smells great. I'm starving." John placed the platter on the table, poured himself a glass of sangria, and sat at the deck table. "I'm exhausted. I've been going all day. I've shown a million houses to this client, but nothing is right." He mimicked the man. "Too many rooms, too few rooms, the layout is boring, the deck is on the wrong side of the house, there's too little landscaping, the landscaping is too complex." He blew out a long breath and shook his head. "I don't know what to do to please this guy. He wants *everything* to be to his liking. Most people buy and then make some alterations to suit them. Maybe this guy should build."

Viv clucked some comforting words about how difficult it could be to work with the public and handed John a plate. "Eat up. You'll feel better. I bet you haven't eaten since breakfast."

John loaded his plate with food. "Come to think of it, I didn't even eat breakfast today."

Viv rolled her eyes and smiled. "You need a nanny to care for you."

The conversation turned to Viv's day at the bookstore, Jeff's new renovation project at his friend Neil's house, and Lin and Leonard's landscaping of Neil's backyard.

John asked where Neil's house was located and when he heard where it was, he said, "I showed a few houses in that area today. What street is the place on?"

Jeff gave the address and John nodded. "I know

Neil's house. In fact, I showed the house next door to a client before I finished for the day."

Lin felt a rush of unease. "Which house? On the right or the left side? I didn't see a "for sale" sign."

John swallowed his bite of burger and said, "The house to the right. The owner refused a sign in front of the house. He huffed about not wanting to advertise that the place was empty. He told me a decent Realtor would be able to sell a house without a sign." Shaking his head, he added, "I didn't say this to the man, but yes, sure, I can bring in some offers, but it would be a lot quicker and smarter to use every method available to spread the word that the house is on the market."

"Has it been for sale long?" Jeff asked. "It's a nice peaceful neighborhood, lots of nice-looking antique houses."

As darkness settled in, a refreshing breeze rustled the leaves at the top of the backyard's trees.

"It's been on the market for a couple of weeks. It's a little run down inside, not updated to today's demands." John added some pasta salad to his plate. "There's the ghost thing, too."

Lin sat up and stared at John, a shiver running over her skin.

Viv took a quick look at Lin and Jeff before asking, "What ghost thing?"

"I've sold plenty of houses that were supposedly haunted," John said.

Lin flinched at the word *haunted*.

"The house is haunted?" Jeff asked. "Lots of places on the island have the reputation that ghosts inhabit them. They always get sold anyway."

"Yeah," John sipped his sangria. "But, this one is supposed to be angry and menacing."

"Who said that about the ghost?" Lin questioned.

"The owner. He's rented the house for years. Most everyone leaves after the lease finishes or they leave before the lease runs out. He told me no one ever renews a lease for that place."

"Really? No one?" Viv found it hard to believe.

"The owner is tired of the endless turnover so he put the place on the market. He said he knows I have a good reputation for moving properties so he hired me because he's afraid no one will want the dang house. Those were his words." John chuckled. "*Dang* house."

"Do you feel a ghost when you're inside?" Lin asked. "Does anything ever happen when you're showing the house?"

John scoffed. He had not yet been told about Lin's ability and did not believe in ghostly apparitions. "Absolutely not. Those tales are just that ... ghost stories. People hear stuff about a ghost in the house, then they start believing every little thing that happens is because of some spirit. They scare themselves and then they want out. It's all in their heads."

Nicky let out a whine.

"I don't know...." Jeff said. "I don't think such things can be dismissed so easily."

John looked at Jeff and raised an eyebrow. "Anyway, this place got the reputation that an angry spirit lives there and lots of people don't want anything to do with it ... which makes my job more difficult ... and unfortunately, I don't get a bigger commission because of the difficulty."

"You didn't have to take the listing." Viv smiled knowing John would never refuse a client.

"Yes, I did have to take it." John laughed. "I consider it a challenge."

Lin wanted to hear more. "Has the owner ever experienced a ghostly event in the house?"

"If he has, he didn't tell me."

"Did you ask him?" Lin pressed.

John thought about the question. "The man told me about the place's reputation. He didn't confide any of his own experiences and I didn't ask. All I needed to know to list the house was that some people think the place is haunted. No testimonials required."

Lin asked another question. "Does the owner think there's some validity about the ghostly presence?"

John shook his head. "He didn't say anything about whether he believes the stories or not."

"The owner doesn't live in the house?" Viv looked pensive.

"No. It's empty. I don't think the guy has ever lived in the house. He's always used it for rental purposes."

"Where does the owner live?" Jeff added some ketchup to his burger.

"In Madaket."

Lin put her fork on the edge of her plate. "Have you heard any specifics about what the ghost does? Why do people think it's angry?"

"Got me," John told her. "The owner stops by the house regularly to check on it. You'll probably see him one day when you're at Neil's working on the landscaping. Go over and ask him what people say about the ghost." John made eye contact with Lin and grinned. "But don't spread around the bad things the owner says about the ghost or I'll never sell the place. Enough people have heard the rumors already."

"If I see the owner, maybe I'll go over to talk to him," Lin said. "It's intriguing. Or if I don't run into the owner, maybe I'll ask the caretaker what he knows about the house."

John looked up blankly. "There's no caretaker."

"Yeah, there is. I met him the other day. A young guy, in his twenties."

John made a face. "Well, no one told me about a caretaker."

"Maybe the owner recently hired him because no one's currently renting the house," Viv said as she reached for the platter of grilled corn on the cob.

"Maybe that's it," Jeff said.

Remembering how the young caretaker seemed to know a few things about her made Lin feel uncomfortable all over again. Maybe when she ran into the owner, she'd ask him about the ghost ... *and* the caretaker.

7

———

L in loaded another shovelful of soil into the wheelbarrow and wiped her sweaty forehead with the back of her hand. The heat and humidity were at full force and she longed to bike to the beach and jump into the ocean. Nicky was inside the air-conditioned house with Jeff and more than once that morning, Lin thought about giving up landscaping altogether and returning full-time to programming where she could sit at her desk, warm in the winter, and cool in the summer.

After pushing the wheelbarrow to the marked-off flower bed's boundary and unloading the loam into it, Lin decided she needed a break, grabbed her water bottle, and walked over to sit in the grass in the shade of a huge Beech tree. Her face felt hot and she bet her cheeks were as red as a beet. From her spot under the tree, she admired the work she and Leonard had already completed. The space was taking shape and, despite having to work in the middle of a heatwave, the landscaping project was ahead of schedule.

Leonard was off handling some of their other clients' yard maintenance and then he was going to come to Neil's place to join Lin and Jeff for lunch and then the two landscapers would tackle some planting of flowering shrubs during the afternoon.

Two hours later, Lin's tank top and jean shorts were drenched in sweat and she sighed with relief when she heard Leonard pull the truck into the long driveway and slam his door.

When he came around the corner of the house, he said, "You look like a drowned rat, Coffin. What did you do, fall into a pond?"

Lin dropped her shovel on the ground and headed across the lawn. "I fell into a vat of my own sweat."

Leonard scowled. "You're disgusting."

"How come you're not covered in grime and perspiration?" Lin eyed her partner. "Have you just been sitting in Viv's bookstore all morning sipping a coffee in the nice cool space while I've been slaving in one-hundred percent humidity?"

"The heat doesn't bother me." Leonard walked to the beds to inspect what Lin had worked on.

"How can the heat not bother you?" Lin trailed after the man. "That's not normal."

"I guess I'm not normal then."

"And the darned humidity." Lin redid her ponytail to capture the loose ends that had fallen out of the elastic. "It's like carrying around a wet blanket over my shoulders. A heavy, gross wet blanket. It's hideous."

"I don't mind it." Leonard picked up the shovel from the grass.

Lin put her hands on her hips and stared at Leonard with puzzled blue eyes. "I swear, there must be something wrong with you."

"You're the one complaining," he said. "Maybe you're the one who has something wrong with her."

"Let's go inside to eat lunch." Lin headed for her truck. "I brought a change of clothes. I knew I'd be drenched."

"Thanks for small favors," Leonard teased. "I won't have to eat lunch with a drowned rat."

LIN FELT REFRESHED after changing clothes and eating lunch with Jeff and Leonard sitting inside in the air-conditioned dining room of Neil's house. The three talked about the day's work and what still needed to be accomplished. Jeff showed them the new kitchen cabinets that were to be installed and they praised the fine craftsmanship and the beauty of the cherry wood.

Lin and Leonard returned to the yard and spent two hours planting the shrubs and mulching part of the beds. When Leonard left to pick up two more hydrangeas, Lin handled the planting of some perennials. She walked to the edge of the driveway where they'd unloaded some of the flowers and carrying the flats back towards the beds, Lin noticed someone in the side yard of the neighbor's house.

Wearing wire-rimmed glasses, the man looked to be in his mid to late-thirties, was clean-shaven, had short brown hair and a slim build. Lin waved to him as she walked over to the property line and when the man saw her approaching, he went over to meet her.

Lin introduced herself, but didn't offer her dirty hand to shake.

"George." The man nodded. "You're working next door?"

Lin explained the job she and Leonard were doing. "Are you the owner?"

George nodded and looked over to the antique Cape. "I've owned the place for years."

Lin said, "I know your real estate agent. I had dinner with him and some friends last night. He mentioned that some people talk about a ghost being in your house."

"My what? What did you say?" The man blinked at her. "A ghost?"

"In the house," Lin said. "Some people say there's a ghost that lives in the house."

The corner of George's mouth turned up and he looked at Lin like she was kidding with him. "Well ... a ghost, is there? I haven't made his acquaintance, as yet."

"You've heard the rumor, though?"

"I haven't, no." He shook his head. "Maybe the rumors are from some late-night tales shared to put a scare into folks."

Lin wondered if the man was playing dumb to dispel the idea of spirits haunting his house. "My friend, John, told me that the house is hard to rent because of the ghost so you decided to sell it."

"Did your friend say that?" George seemed

bemused. "I never lease the house, perhaps that's the real reason it's not easy to rent."

Lin was befuddled by the conversation. "You're the owner, right?"

"I am, indeed, along with my wife."

"Does your wife ever talk about a ghost in the house?" Lin asked.

The man chuckled. "My, no, she wouldn't like that one bit. I don't believe she'd set foot in a house with a ghost."

Lin considered for a moment that maybe she and John had been talking about two different houses.

"Why so much interest in my house?" George asked.

"I like it. I've been working here," Lin gestured to Neil's backyard. "I was admiring your place. I heard that some people think there's a ghost inside. I thought it was intriguing."

George smiled kindly. "Well, I am sorry to disappoint you, but there is no spirit keeping company within those walls. Your friends must be talking about a different house or maybe they're playing a prank on you."

"I talked to your maintenance man the other day," Lin began.

George's eyebrow raised as he scrunched his face in confusion. "My maintenance man?"

"Yes. He was working here a couple of days ago. I had a short chat with him."

"A man was working here?" The man's face became serious.

Lin nodded. "I don't know his name. I'm not sure if he told me his name or maybe I didn't hear it."

"We don't employ a man."

Lin's mouth opened, but she didn't know what to say, so she put her lips together.

"I don't know who you could mean," George told her.

A rush of adrenaline ran through Lin's veins from confusion and anxiety. "He was in his early twenties, maybe mid-twenties. He was pleasant. Dark hair. He said he was the maintenance man."

"Maybe he works for the owners of the house on the far side of that one," the man pointed to Neil's house. "Maybe the neighbors on the other side employ a man to take care of their property."

Lin heard Leonard's truck coming into the driveway. "My partner is back. Maybe we can talk another time?"

"That would be very nice." George nodded and headed for the rear of his property.

Lin shook her head, thinking for a minute that she might be turning crazy from the heat.

"Slacking off again, Coffin?" Leonard unloaded some shrubs from the rear of his truck.

"I had the oddest conversation with the man next door." Lin looked back over her shoulder.

"Maybe you shouldn't talk to strangers." Leonard lifted a large burning bush from the truck bed and set it down at the end of the driveway. "Especially when you're supposed to be working."

"Don't you want to know why the conversation was odd?" Lin asked.

"Nope." Leonard hoisted a bush and headed away to the bed they'd been working on. "We got work to do."

Lin pulled her phone from her bag of tools and texted John asking which house was the one he had listed that had a ghost in it. While waiting for John's reply, she lifted one of the hydrangeas and heaved it over to the new bed.

When her phone buzzed, she took a look at John's answer.

If you're facing Neil's house, it's the Cape to the right.

Lin stared at the message. The house John held the listing for was the same house where she'd met the caretaker and where she'd just talked to the owner. A shiver ran down Lin's back. Both John and the owner claimed there was no caretaker working at the house. John said people talk about a ghost in the home, but the owner claimed that a ghost in his house is only a silly story someone made up to frighten people.

Lin scratched her head. *What's going on?*

8

In the late afternoon sunshine, Lin and Viv walked down the wooden staircase from the top of the cliff where they'd left their bikes. The sparkling, blue ocean of Nantucket Sound stretched out below and beyond them into the distance all the way to the mainland of Massachusetts. The expansive view never failed to take Lin's breath away.

The gorgeous white sand of the beach was soft and fine, green vegetation grew in the dunes, sails of boats dotted the sea, and the sky met the ocean way on the horizon. Every time they came to Step's Beach, Lin had to stand at the top of the staircase for a minute before descending, needing a few moments to revel in the beauty that spread out before her.

As soon as they dropped their towels on the sand, the young women raced each other into the water where they swam way out and bobbed in the calm, cool, refreshing ocean.

"So tell me more about the owner of the house next door to Neil's," Viv said floating on her back in the water with her sunglasses on.

Switching between treading water and floating, Lin told her cousin about the exchange she had with George, the owner of the Cape. "Maybe I was addled by the heat and didn't understand him correctly."

Viv lifted her sunglasses and eyed Lin for a second. "The heat didn't cause any confusion. Ole George is trying to take the focus off the ghost by poo-pooing the idea that a spirit is real. He's all about selling the house so he makes light of the stories that a ghost lives in the place."

"Maybe you're right."

"I'm always right," Viv kidded.

Lin thought over what George had said to her. "What about the caretaker guy?"

Viv rolled off her back and treaded water next to her cousin. "I think the guy may have been telling you a fib about being a caretaker. Either he was walking around the property to give it a look before deciding if he wanted John to show it to him or he was casing the house to break in at a later date."

Lin's eyes went wide. "A robber, huh? I didn't think of that. And you're right about the other option, the young guy might have been interested in buying the place, but wanted to look around the outside of the house before making a commitment to see it with a Realtor. When I approached him, he must have made up the story about being the caretaker."

Viv and Lin swam further out from the beach in the cool, clear water.

"I needed this. It was so hot and humid today, I almost felt sick." Lin dove under the small waves and surfaced a few yards from Viv.

"The bookstore was crazy today." Viv pushed her wet hair off of her forehead. "Even though I don't work outside in the heat, I felt overworked and harried so when you suggested a swim, I jumped on it. I feel much better now." Treading water, she asked, "Have you seen the old ghost again who was in your kitchen the other night?"

"I haven't." Lin's voice was sad. "If he doesn't materialize for me, I don't know how I'll figure out what he wants."

"It could be that the ghost wanted validation of

some sort. Maybe you appeased him with what you said."

Lin gave a scowl. "I promised him I'd figure out what he needed. He can't just up and disappear and never come back. He can't just leave it to me. I need some help here."

"Your clever cousin is by your side." Viv saluted.

Lin smiled. "We *both* need some help here."

The two decided to head back and warm themselves on the sand so they struck out for the shore, their swimming strokes relaxed and easy as their arms dipped and rose in the water. When they reached the beach, the young women toweled off and sat in the sun for a while enjoying the view.

"I'm starving," Viv announced. "Let's ride over to Cliff Road to the sandwich shop."

Lin agreed. They pulled on shorts and tank tops, took their towels, and climbed the stairs up to the top of the dunes to their bikes with Viv complaining that there should be an elevator or an escalator to carry people back to the top after their swims. "We just get hot all over again."

After riding the short distance to the sandwich place, the girls ordered and then settled down at a picnic table under the shade of the trees to eat.

"Hey, you two." John, dressed in a linen suit, strode across the lawn to them.

Surprised to see her boyfriend, Viv patted the bench for John to sit next to her. "What are you up to? What are you doing here?"

"I'm meeting a client. I'm showing her a house a few streets over. She asked if I'd meet her here."

Viv gave John part of her sandwich and he munched. "I'm glad I ran into you," he grinned enjoying the delicious snack. He asked Lin, "What happened after I texted you? Did you see the owner of the Cape house?"

"I did." Lin wiped a bit of aioli from her lips. She told him about the conversation she had with the man.

"So he said he didn't employ a caretaker?" John asked.

"That's right."

John said, "Good, because he didn't tell me he had a man taking care of the place. I like to know who's supposed to be around the house and who isn't. Did you ask him about the ghost?"

Lin gave a nod. "He said those were only silly stories that a ghost lived in his house."

John narrowed his eyes. "Really ... because he told me there was a ghost."

Viv sipped from her soft drink. "The owner might have thought Lin was interested in the house or maybe that she had a friend who might be interested. He doesn't want to scare anyone off from a possible sale."

"He can't be telling people there's no ghost. I need to be upfront with the clients I show the place to."

"You actually come right out and say, there's a ghost living in here?" Lin was astounded.

John shook his head. "No, no. I mention, with a smile of course, that some people have suggested the sensation of a ghost around the house. I tell possible buyers, but downplay the unusual news. And I don't want to hear any weird stories of people's experiences who have lived in the house, that way, I can stay neutral. I don't offend anyone who might believe in such things and I don't scare anyone off. It's a delicate balance."

"*I* want to hear the stories about the ghost," Lin told John.

Viv looked up from her sandwich and asked John, "Do you know anyone who's actually spent time living in the Cape?"

John picked up a potato chip from Viv's brown paper sandwich box. "Of course, I do. In fact, the woman I'm meeting here rented that house a few years ago."

Lin almost dropped her sandwich. "She did? Can I talk to her before you leave to show her your listing?"

"I guess so. I'll ask her when she shows up." John gave Lin a look that said he wasn't sure why anyone would want to talk with somebody about a haunted house. "There she is." He stood up, waved, and walked over to his client.

The woman was in her thirties with chin-length, light brown hair. She glanced over to the picnic table and eyed the cousins as John had a few words with her.

John led her over to the table and made introductions. "This is Ginny Hillsborough. She's agreed to chat with you for a few minutes. I'm going to go buy a couple of bottles of water. I'll be back in a few minutes."

Ginny sat down with the cousins. "Nice to meet you. You want to ask about the haunted house?"

"Thanks for agreeing to chat," Lin said. "Can you tell us what you experienced while renting the Cape?"

Ginny let out a sigh. "My husband, he was my boyfriend at the time, and I lived in the house for a year. It was less than that, really, because we moved out two months before the lease was up. We didn't want to stay there anymore. We'd had enough. I've never experienced anything like what went on in that house." Ginny passed her hand over her eyes. "And I hope I never do again."

"What went on?" Viv asked softly, looking horrified to have to engage in the topic of conversation.

"At first, it was little things. Things were moved from where we left them. Doors slammed shut. Lights came on in rooms without us flicking the lamps on." Ginny paused in her telling. "Cold air, freezing air, would float through the room like we'd left the door open in the middle of a winter night. Colder than that, actually."

"Did you ever see anything?" Lin asked.

"We saw lights moving through the hallway at night sometimes. A glowing ball." She held her hands to show the size … which was a little bigger than a baseball.

"Was that why you moved out?" Viv questioned.

Ginny made eye contact with Viv and Lin. "No, it wasn't. The things I told you about were odd enough, but other things were the reason we left." She sucked in a breath. "Some nights we'd wake up to the sound of sobbing. Terrible sobbing. A man's cries."

"Where was it coming from?" Viv rubbed the goosebumps on her arms.

"We could never pinpoint it. Sometimes when the man was crying, he called out a name … it was hard to make out, it sounded like Sara, or Clara, or something like that. It was chilling." Ginny shuddered. "You can't imagine."

Lin thought she probably could imagine.

"Someone mentioned to John that the ghost seemed angry," Viv said. "Did you ever get that impression?"

Ginny nodded gravely. "We did, yes. It was more than an impression. You might think we're crazy, believing these things happened, but some nights after the crying, objects in our room would get picked up and thrown across the bedroom."

Viv gasped.

"Did the objects move on their own?" Lin's eyes were like saucers.

"It seemed like they were being lifted and thrown by an invisible hand. We'd be in bed and the room would fill with freezing air. We knew if that happened right after the sobbing stopped that something would go airborne in a minute or two." Ginny crossed her arms over her chest. "It was unnerving, let me tell you."

"Did you feel like you were in danger?" Lin asked.

"Not really. The spirit never seemed to be after *us*. It seemed like the ghost was full of terrible sorrow and anger that was directed at someone, but not towards us." Ginny checked her watch. "I should get going to see the house John wants to show me. I don't have a lot of time today."

Lin saw John standing in the parking lot next to his car. She thought of one more question to ask. "What made you decide to leave the house? Was it a build-up of a lot of things or did something happen in particular that made you want to get out?"

"I found out I was pregnant. The crying and the freezing air and the breaking things increased. Once in the middle of the night, my husband got up to use the bathroom and when he came back to the bedroom, he got hit in the head with a flying book. It wasn't intended for him, at least, we didn't think so. It was just another ghostly fit being had. My husband decided he didn't want me getting hurt by stepping into the path of something being thrown. I agreed with him that it was time to get out of there. We don't usually tell people about what went on in that house. Most people looked at us like we were nuts when we discussed it, so we decided to keep the experience to ourselves." Ginny looked over to John and nodded. "John said it was okay to talk to you about it. If he didn't vouch for you, I would never have agreed."

Lin and Viv thanked the woman for sharing and Ginny started away, but stopped and turned back. "You know, talking about it has made me sad all over again. That poor spirit or ghost or whatever it is that's stuck inside that house, when we lived there, I wished so much that I could help him. It just about broke my heart listening to that terrible sobbing."

Lin swallowed hard. She was pretty sure she knew who the sorrowful, angry ghost was who lived in that Cape house.

9

———

Lin stepped over the threshold into the gray-shingled antique Cape on the lot next to Neil's place. The sun had set and darkness settled over the yard and invaded the spaces of the house. The floor creaked when she walked across the living room to admire a huge stone fireplace. The ceilings were lower than in modern houses, but Lin thought it gave the room a cozy feeling.

John flicked the wall switch and the light came on and chased away the shadows.

Lin and Viv met John at the house so they could get a sense of the home. They told him that Lin could spread the word about the place being for sale to some of her landscaping clients who might enjoy stories of ghosts or who believed that ghosts moved among the living.

"Have a look around the place and spread the word to your customers," John encouraged. "I'm going to sit in the car and make some calls to my clients."

The Cape had been nicely kept up and the wide pine floors were in good shape for being over two-hundred-and fifty-years old. As the cousins moved from the living room, to the dining room, and into the kitchen, Viv remarked how surprisingly large the rooms were for such an old house. There were two bedrooms and a sunroom on the first floor as well as two bathrooms.

"This is a great house for a family," Viv said while standing in front of the wall of windows in the sunroom. "So roomy and with a beautiful backyard." Turning to her cousin, she watched Lin walk around the room, running her hand over a few of the furniture pieces remaining in the house. "Are you picking up on anything?" Viv asked.

"Not yet," Lin said quietly. There was a strange silence in the house. It felt ... empty, lonely. Lin's heart contracted. She moved to a door on the other side of the kitchen and as she reached for the latch, a vibrating humming sensation moved over her skin. She pulled her hand back.

"Is that a closet?" Viv asked.

"I think it's the door to the back staircase." Lin's heart pounded. She placed the palm of her hand on the wooden door and a buzzing pulsed against her skin. Moving her hand to the left, she grasped the latch and pulled the door open.

A dark whoosh of bad feelings rushed from the narrow stairwell and almost knocked Lin over.

"Are you going up?" Viv didn't realize that her cousin was picking up on things floating on the air and she came behind Lin and peeked up the stairs.

"Um, maybe we should use the main staircase." Lin did not want to go up to the second floor using the back stairs.

"Why?" Viv questioned.

"The steps look a little rickety." Lin backed away and shut the door, letting the latch click into place.

Viv led the way to the front of the house and started up the steps. Lin took in a breath and followed. At the top of the landing, there was a long hallway with four bedrooms, a bathroom, and a small room that had probably been most recently used as an office. The back staircase was at the end of the hall.

Lin got a dark feeling in her chest when she approached the door to the stairs. It made her shudder and want to hurry away. Again, she forced herself to place her palm against the door and felt the same buzzing and pricking against her skin that she experienced on the first floor when looking at the staircase. It was as if the vibration was warning her to get away.

"I feel something bad," Lin whispered.

Viv's breath caught in her throat and she practically ran to Lin's side. "Bad? What kind of bad?"

"I don't know. I feel it near the back staircase."

Viv laced her arm through Lin's and tugged. "Get away from it then. Let's go downstairs. Let's use the main staircase."

"I'd like to stand here for a minute."

Viv stood still flicking her eyes around the space, her chest rapidly rising and falling with shallow breaths. "For only one minute, then we're out of here."

Long ago impressions moved in the air, some bumped against Lin, while others floated gently past. She attempted to steady herself by deepening her breathing and relaxing her muscles and she listened to the vibrations that lingered in the long-ago atmosphere of the house. Snippets of things washed over her ... joy and love, and then a feeling of sadness.

Suddenly, a sensation hit Lin square in the chest and almost made her fall back. It was a sucker-punch of terror and fear followed by disbelief, and then crushing grief, misery, and the longing for something that was no more.

Lin inhaled audibly and took three steps back.

"What is it? What's happening?" Viv grabbed her cousin's arm. "Are you okay?"

Lin gave a nod and moved her hand to her temple. "Let's go now."

After reaching the first floor of the house, the young women sat at the old wooden kitchen table.

"Did you see a ghost?" Viv asked, her face pale.

With her shoulders hunched, Lin looked worn out. "I didn't. I didn't feel any cold air. I didn't see anything." She rested her elbows on the tabletop and held her head in her hands.

"Why did you gasp then? You must have seen *something*."

"It was sensations, feelings ... impressions." Lin looked into her cousin's eyes. "There were happy times in this house ... then something bad happened, maybe two bad things. I feel it most at the back stairs."

Viv moved her hand to her throat. "Did someone get murdered in here?"

"I don't know what happened." Lin gave a sad half-smile. "I don't really know what the sensations are."

"Was it an accident of some sort? Did someone break in? Did someone get killed?"

"What happened here a long time ago feels terribly, terribly sad." Lin shrugged. "Whatever it was."

"Why doesn't that old ghost show up?" Viv glanced over her shoulders as if she was concerned that the spirit would sneak up on them. "If he wants help, he needs to show up and point us to some clues."

Lin gave a weary shrug. Being in the house seemed to be sapping her energy.

Viv sat up straight. "Did the old ghost live here? Can you sense his presence in this house? Maybe he never lived here at all. Maybe being here isn't going to help at all."

"I don't know who I sense." Lin's voice was small. "I've only seen the old ghost once. I don't have a good sense of him. I don't know if he lived here or not. I don't know if the sadness in this house is connected to him or to someone else."

"If he did live here as a ghost, where did he go?" Viv pulled her chair closer to the table.

Lin frowned. "You know I don't understand a single thing about this skill of mine. I also don't know a single thing about ghosts."

"You know a few things," Viv reminded her cousin. "You know they never speak."

"What else do I know?" Lin looked exhausted.

Viv's lips squeezed together in a tight line while she thought about what else Lin knew. "Well, I can't think of anything right this second, but there must be something else."

"Why don't we head out?" Disappointment from not finding out anything about the ghost was evident in Lin's tone.

Before they got out of their seats, the back door opened with a bang and Lin and Viv leapt to their feet.

John stepped into the room holding a flashlight and saw the startled looks on the girls' faces. "Sorry, a gust of wind pulled the door right out of my grasp."

"Why are you coming in through the back?" Viv asked.

"I walked around the outside of the house to be sure everything was okay. There's no moon. It's really dark." John looked from Viv to Lin. "You all done? We ready to get going?"

The cousins nodded and John locked the back door. Walking through the living room to the front, John chuckled. "Did you run into any ghosts while you were touring the house?"

"Only one," Viv kidded her boyfriend. "He told me to warn you to never be in this house alone."

John spun around and stared at Viv and she let out a hoot of laughter. "I thought you didn't believe in ghosts."

With a scowl, John led the way to the front door muttering how Viv's joke wasn't funny at all.

Smiling at Viv's light-hearted teasing of her boyfriend, Lin took a last look around the living room before following the others out of the house.

Something on the empty bookshelf in the corner of the room caught Lin's attention. She narrowed her eyes and her heart raced. A sailor's valentine stood on the middle shelf. It looked exactly like the one she'd bought at the shop the other day.

"Lin?" John poked his head around the corner.

"I'm coming. I was looking at something. I'll be right there."

John gave a nod and when he stepped into the small foyer, Lin turned back to the bookshelf.

Her eyes went wide and she blinked several times.

There was nothing on the shelf. Every one of the shelves was empty.

The valentine was gone.

10

With her eyes blurring, Lin sat hunched by the windows of the research room reading information online through the town library system. She'd already studied books and articles on sailor's valentines and had turned next to investigate old land records trying to trace the former owners of the antique Cape.

Viv hurried over to Lin's table and pulled up a chair next to her. "Mallory's watching the bookstore until I get back. What have you found?"

"I read what I could find about the valentines and I found the land records going back to the 1800s. I assume that's when our ghost lived since that was the time when the sailors traveled and purchased the valentines. Not all the records have street names that match up with today, but I think this land plot description is the one that indicates the antique Cape house." She pointed to the computer screen so Viv could see.

Viv squinted at the screen. "Okay, that looks right."

Lin switched to a page of deed listings. "The names of the sellers and the buyers are listed here along with the page number in the deed book. Here are the owners of that house during the 1800s." Each name had been handwritten in the book's pages.

Lin pointed to each one as she read them aloud. "1810-1830, E.G. North, 1830-1836, G.W. Weeks, 1836-1866, Roger Ethan, and 1866-1908, Matthew Whitaker." Turning to face her cousin, Lin said, "Matthew Whitaker is probably not our ghost. I think the ghost is someone who lived in the early 1800s because that's when the majority of the valentines were bought in Barbados and carried back to Nantucket. So, I think that E.G. North or G.W. Weeks is our man."

"Terrific sleuthing." Viv was impressed with Lin's ability to wade through so much material to match up the history of the time with the possible owner of the house.

"I'm going with the idea that our ghost sailed in the early part of the nineteenth century as a young man. From what I've read, a lot of the sailors tired of being away from home for a year at a time on each voyage and after a few trips, they left sailing to find other work somewhere on the island or ended up moving to the mainland." Lin rubbed at her eyes. "I'm done for the day. My eyes are going to fall out if I try to read one more thing." She closed out of the library computer, gathered her things, and left the building with Viv.

They walked the few blocks through town to Viv's neighborhood, turned down her lane, and reaching the house with the white picket fence covered with blooming roses, opened the gate to the walkway and headed inside where Queenie and Nicky greeted them with sleepy eyes.

"Must be nice to nap all afternoon," Viv told the animals.

"They're the house security guards." Lin reached down to give the dog and cat some pats.

"We'd better get changed. John and Jeff will be here any minute." Viv headed up to her room to change into biking shorts and a top. The foursome had planned a late afternoon bike ride around the island, dinner at a pub down by the docks, and then dessert back at Viv's house on the deck.

Lin needed to get the kinks out of her neck and looked forward to the brisk exercise riding along the island bike paths. When the guys arrived, the cousins were outside ready to go.

John asked, "Can we start out by going over to the Polpis Road? I have some paperwork I told the owner of the antique Cape I'd drop in his mailbox by tonight."

The four set out for the paths by biking up Viv's road, cutting through a cemetery, and hooking into the bicycle trails that would lead along Milestone Road to Polpis.

The humidity had cleared out and the air felt fresh and warm as they pedaled past gray-shingled cottages, marshes, and meadows. When they reached the Cape house, John took the envelope from his pack and placed it in the mailbox.

Viv suggested biking to Shimmo and then along the Nantucket harbor out to Potter's Point, and then back to the paths that would lead to 'Sconset.

"I haven't been out to Potter's Point since I was little," Lin told them.

"I never bike that way," Jeff said. "Good idea, Viv."

Off they went along the wooded areas, past fields and pastureland, to the small road that wove by the harbor, bent inland for a few miles, and then led back beside the harbor again. The breeze felt good on Lin's face as the group moved along at a good speed, but when the road got closer to Potter's Point, a wave of anxiety flashed through her and she wished they'd gone on an alternate route.

"I think we should head this way," John gestured. "It will take us back to the Polpis Road."

After several miles, Viv requested a break for water so they pulled to the side and reached for their bottles.

"My legs are tired already," Viv worried. "I don't know if I can make the whole circuit."

"You'll be okay," Jeff encouraged. "Maybe your legs will loosen up after the next couple of miles."

Viv's expression told Jeff that she didn't think that would happen. "I'll go a little further, but I might abandon all of you and head back to town taking a shorter route."

Being in the area of Potter's Point was making Lin uneasy and she offered to return to town with Viv if she didn't feel up to the entire planned ride. After two more miles, Viv decided to bow out, so she and Lin left the men to complete the ride around the island with the plan to meet back at Viv's where they would change and head to the docks for dinner.

When Jeff and John pedaled away, Lin looked at her cousin. "I feel weird."

Viv's lips turned down. "Tired weird or paranormal weird?"

"Not tired," Lin said glumly.

"Oh," Viv whispered and glanced over her shoulders. "Maybe we should have stayed with the guys?"

"It's okay. As soon as we rode closer to the point, the feeling started up."

"Are we in danger?" Viv's eyes were big.

Lin waved her hand around. "No. I'm picking up on something ... whatever it is." She let out a breath. "Come on. Let's get going."

"I think this might be a shortcut back to the paths that run along the main road." Viv led the way down the shady, wooded area until the space opened up and they emerged closer to the water. "This way," Viv turned her bike down a quiet lane.

The lane ended in a dead end.

"Wrong way. About face." Viv shrugged.

"What's all that?" Lin pointed to mounds and mounds of white shells in an empty lot that bordered the harbor.

"It looks like a place where they dump the scallop shells."

"It's huge," Lin said, an odd sensation fluttering over her skin. "I didn't know shells got dumped out and left in big piles."

"The fishermen used to dump loads of shells. Some of the piles on the island started in the late 1700s. I don't know if this pile is old or if it's still being used."

Lin couldn't pull her eyes away from the sight. Piles of white shells, most of them crushed, others intact, shimmered in the early evening sunlight.

Viv narrowed her eyes at her cousin. "You want to go look at them?"

"What?" Lin looked deep in thought as she turned to Viv.

"Want to ride down and get a closer look?"

"No." Lin almost shouted.

"What's wrong with you?" Viv asked.

"Nothing." Lin took a quick glance to the scallop shell piles.

Viv raised an eyebrow. "Nothing, huh?"

"You know I said I had a weird feeling?" Lin's breathing was fast and shallow. "I think it's coming from down near the shells."

"Should we have a look?"

"I guess so." Lin gave a reluctant, little nod so they walked their bikes along the path to the shell mounds where they could see the water of the harbor glittering beyond.

Lin's vision began to swim and the dizziness caused her to become unsteady. A feeling of sadness hit her in the chest like a fast-pitched baseball and she staggered back. "I need to get out of here," she whispered.

With one hand on her bike's handlebars, Viv placed her other hand on Lin's arm to help support her. When they'd reached the lane they'd arrived on, Lin's sensations of alarm waned. She swigged from her water bottle and then poured some into her hand and splashed it on her face. "I'm starting to feel better."

"Can you make it home?" Viv's voice sounded worried.

"I'll be okay." Lin swung her leg over her bike and started to pedal. "Let's get the heck away from here."

11

After arriving back at Viv's house, the young women showered and changed and went out for dinner with Jeff and John. Being far away from the shell mounds, the anxious sensations quickly disappeared and Lin ended up feeling silly for having the unsettling moments of anxiety while observing the shells.

Feeling foolish about it, she didn't share with the men what had come over her when she and Viv viewed the unusual sight of the discarded scallop shells. "I've been so caught up thinking about the old ghost and the antique Cape house that seeing something unexpected and out of the ordinary sort of knocked me for a loop." She apologized to her cousin for behaving so weirdly, but Viv pooh-poohed the expression of regret.

"We all act kooky every once in a while." Viv tapped her index finger against her chin and said kiddingly, "Although, I can't remember the last time *I* acted oddly ... it was so very long ago."

Lin leveled her eyes at her cousin. "Shall I remind you of the last time you behaved like a kook?"

"Nope." Viv smiled and went into the kitchen leaving Lin, the cat, and the dog in the living room looking after her as she exited.

Lin made eye contact with the animals. "She got out of that one, didn't she?"

When Lin, Jeff, Viv, and John returned to the house after having dinner, they all sat outside on the deck with drinks to share the dessert Viv had made. Candles flickered on the table and the evening air was warm and pleasant. Nicky and Queenie rested in the grass watching fireflies dart about the backyard.

Viv had gone all out making an English trifle and the guests reported on how delicious the sweet concoction tasted. John and Jeff had two helpings each.

"I can't stuff another bite into my stomach." Lin

leaned back in her chair with her hands on her abdomen. "Although, I'd love to eat that whole thing."

After good company and good food, Lin's unease had faded away and she was able to think about the shell mounds without any anxiety flaring up. The small group played cards for an hour after eating dessert and then everyone groaned about having to get up early the next morning while helping Viv with the dishes.

When Lin and Nicky arrived back at home, she walked quickly to the hutch to take a look at the sailor's valentine. She ran her hand over the glass top of the wooden box and said softly, "What does your ghost need from me?"

The box did not give off any heat when Lin touched it. The valentine hadn't been hot to the touch since the night she'd brought it home and now, it seemed to be just a normal, household decoration.

Lin yawned mightily, got ready for bed, snuggled under the covers in her cool, air-conditioned bedroom, reached for her crossword puzzle book, and filled in two answers before nodding off.

THE BEDSIDE LAMP was still on and the puzzle book was next to her on the blanket when she woke up to birds singing their early-morning wake-up songs and Lin marveled at how quickly sunrise had come.

She and Nicky rode in the truck to pick up Leonard whose own vehicle had gone into the shop for service. Lin parked at the end of his crushed-shell driveway and she and the dog walked up the three steps to the front door of the pretty Cape house. Lin rang the bell three times, but no one answered, and becoming concerned, she and her canine companion walked around to the rear of the house to knock on the back door.

"Leonard?" Lin gave a couple of raps on the door's glass window.

"I overslept, Coffin," Leonard called from some-where inside. "I just got out of the shower. Wait for me in your truck. I'll be right there."

Lin and Nicky walked back to the truck. Not being invited into the house to wait in Leonard's kitchen brought back the question of why the man was unable to have anyone in his home. Being made to wait outside also hurt Lin's feelings.

With wet hair, Leonard burst through the front door carrying his lunchbox and saw Lin leaning against her truck. "I'm ready."

"I'm not." Lin locked eyes with the older man.

"What's wrong with you? I made us late. We don't need to be later. Let's get a move on." Leonard went to the passenger side. Nicky was sitting beside the truck. He didn't give Leonard his usual joyous greeting.

The man looked down at the brown dog and made a face. "What's wrong with you?"

When Nicky didn't move, Leonard turned back to Lin. "What's going on?"

"Exactly." Lin, with her eyes dark and her face pinched, took some steps closer.

With a scowl on his face, Leonard let out a long, exasperated breath. "What?"

"We're business partners, but first and more importantly, I consider us friends," Lin began. "I hope you feel the same way."

"Is this true confessions, or something?"

Lin cocked her head and said gently, "It could be, if you'd fess up to why you never invite me into your home."

Leonard's eyes widened and his face muscles drooped. He couldn't joke his way out of the comment. "I was in a hurry … the house is a mess...."

Lin held her hand up. "I'm not buying it. You deliberately keep me out."

"I do not."

"You've been to my house a million times. You've had lunch and dinner and even breakfast in my house. You drop by unannounced and I invite you in."

Leonard ran his hand over the top of his head. "It's just never a convenient time when you're here."

"What's the real reason?" Lin asked.

"That *is* the reason."

Lin sighed. "Leonard...."

"I don't like people seeing a messy house."

Lin said, "My house is messy when you've been over."

"It's a tic of mine. Things have to be neat." Leonard stepped around the dog and opened the passenger side door. "We're late. We need to get going."

Lin stared at the man with a look of disappointment.

"Can I go in and use your bathroom?"

"Coffin...."

"Forget it." Lin strode to the truck, opened the door, and got in. She turned the ignition while Leonard reached down, lifted the dog into the truck's cab, and got in himself.

They drove for two miles with neither one saying a word.

Leonard said softly, "Don't be mad."

"I'm not angry," Lin muttered. "I'm hurt."

Leonard let out a groan. "Don't be hurt, for Pete's sake. It doesn't have anything to do with you."

"What *does* it have to do with?" Lin kept her eyes on the road.

Leonard remained silent.

Lin turned the truck down a side street. "I wish you'd tell me."

The older man watched out of his window for a full minute, before saying, mostly to himself, "I just can't tell you."

When they arrived at their client's home, Lin and Leonard went separate ways to mow the lawn, weed flower beds, and trim the hedges. The hour and a half dragged by without the easy, fun, comfortable banter between the two landscapers.

Leonard paused in the shade with his bottle of water and as Lin walked by on her way to get a tool, he asked, trying to thaw things out between them, "How was your bike ride last night?"

"It was okay."

"Just okay? Not great?"

"Viv got tired and I...." Lin hesitated.

One of Leonard's eyebrows went up in question. "You, what?"

"Viv and I rode on a deserted lane trying to take a shortcut back to the bike paths. We came up on this spot with mounds and mounds of mostly crushed scallop shells." Lin felt the queasiness from the night before. "It made me want to get out of there."

"Why?"

"It made me feel uncomfortable. I don't know why." Lin cut their conversation short, got the tool she wanted, and headed back to work on one of the flower beds.

Another half hour passed and they'd almost finished the yard when Leonard approached Lin who was kneeling at a flower bed pulling out weeds. "What was it about those shells that made you feel funny?" he asked.

Lin sat back on her heels. "I don't know. It might have been the mood I was in. I was feeling tired, not physically, but sort of mentally drained and the sun was glinting off the white shells. It was too bright. There were too many shells. It didn't seem right. It hurt my eyes."

Leonard stood over Lin looking down at her. He

seemed to be thinking something over. "Yeah," was all he finally said.

A corner of Lin's mouth turned up. "Yeah? The same thing has happened to you? Too many white shells in a pile? The white hot sun beating down on them, blinding you?"

"Yeah." With the toe of his boot, Leonard poked at an old acorn that was pressed into the grass. "Don't be mad at me, Coffin. It makes me feel bad."

Lin was about to say something smart-alecky, when Leonard added, "And don't be hurt, either. It's not my intention to hurt you."

He started to cross the yard to gather up the tools so they could move on to the next client's place. "One of these days, I'll tell you why you don't get asked into my house."

Lin sat back on the grass and watched the man walk across the yard ... and Nicky got up and trotted after Leonard wagging his little tail.

All was forgiven.

12

I t was early evening and Viv and Anton sat at a
small table in the bookstore café listening to
Lin talk about her day with Leonard. "I was
really annoyed with him because he has never once
let me into his house, not even for a minute. He told
me to go wait in the truck. I felt terribly hurt, like I
thought we were friends, but maybe he didn't feel
the same way. I almost cried."

"What happened?" Viv asked. "Did he let you
inside?"

"No, he didn't. He kept making up stupid excuses
about why I couldn't go in."

"Perhaps, the man is simply private." Anton
came to Leonard's defense. "Some people don't like
to entertain. Some people feel their home is a safe

place where they can be themselves. Leonard lost his wife. He struggled for years to cope. The man could barely keep a job and went off the deep end every year around the anniversary of his wife's accident. It could be that Leonard's home is his sanctuary, a sentimental place he has trouble sharing with others." Anton sipped from his tea cup. "He's only recently been able to pull himself together. I don't see him often and I don't know him well, but I don't believe I have ever seen the man in better spirits."

Anton looked over his glasses at Lin. "I believe your friendship and belief in Leonard has pulled him out of a pit of despair and placed him back in the land of the living."

Lin swallowed. She'd never considered she'd done anything important for Leonard.

"Give the man time," Anton clucked. "His late wife, Marguerite, loved that cottage of theirs. I knew her, a lovely person." The historian sighed.

"So did you stay angry with him?" Viv asked.

"Most of the morning I did. Nicky was acting stand-offish with Leonard, too." Lin thought back on the morning. "Leonard tried to start up a conversation. I answered kind of cooly. I was drowning in my own hurt feelings. Later, he asked me about our bike ride. I told him about the shells and said they made me uneasy." Lin looked across the room, thinking. "He got really quiet. Then he said that one day, he would tell me why I was never asked into his home."

Viv sat up. "Really? He'll tell you someday? Wow."

Lin's eyes got misty. "He told me he never wanted to hurt me."

Viv put her hand on her heart. "Gosh. Leonard. He is a very kind man."

"It got me thinking," Lin said. "I was almost ready to toss our friendship aside. I know it was a dumb way to think, but I was hurt and I didn't think our friendship meant anything to him. I felt like it was only me who cared about him. I'm glad I didn't say anything stupid. I'm glad I didn't ruin our relationship because I could only see how things were impacting me. I didn't take the time to consider that Leonard had some sort of personal reason for keeping me out of his house. I took it as a slight when I should have been thinking about Leonard."

"I think we all do that at times." Viv rubbed her forehead. "I wonder how many relationships get ruined because of perceived slights."

"Plenty." Anton looked miserable.

"Is something wrong, Anton?" Viv asked.

Anton's shoulders stooped and his facial muscles

drooped. "The conversation has reminded me of something. Long ago, I lost a very good friend over my own selfish behavior."

"What happened?" Lin questioned.

Anton shook his head. "Oh, it was a lifetime ago. I was a young professor. This other man was an academic, as well. I let my ego get the best of me. I thought this man stole an idea from me. It was utter nonsense on my part. If I'd taken the time to have a rational conversation with him about it, things wouldn't have gone as they did." Anton batted at the air with his hand. "I lost a good friend because I let my hurt and arrogance lead the way. Oh, how wonderful it would be, if we could take back angry words." Looking down at his empty cup, he said softly, "I still miss the man's friendship, even to this day."

The three sat in silence for a few minutes, until Viv gave herself a shake. "Enough of gloomy topics. Let us take a valuable lesson from all of this ... to treat our friendships with the care they deserve." She winked at her cousin and smiled. "Even our friendships with family members."

Lin chuckled, and kidded, "Those being the most difficult friendships of all."

Viv reached over and playfully batted her

cousin's arm. "I need to help Mallory clean up." She looked at Anton. "Stay until we lock up, if you like." Viv stood and then turned back to Lin. "Could you do me a favor? Could you make a deposit at the ATM for me?"

"Now?" Lin asked.

"Could you? I have some cash I'd like to get into the account as soon as possible."

"Of course." Lin reached for her wallet and phone and glanced over to the dog and cat sleeping in the easy chair together. "I'll leave the snooze-hound here while I run the errand."

The streets of town bustled with tourists and locals strolling the brick sidewalks and cobblestone roads to restaurants and shops, and down to the docks to ogle the boats and yachts. The old-fashioned streetlamps started to glimmer over the town and it was easy to imagine living in early nineteenth-century Nantucket.

Lin took a short-cut to the bank and approached the shop where she'd purchased the sailor's valentine. Passing by, she peered in the windows and, distracted, almost plowed into a man standing on the sidewalk outside of the neighboring store.

"I'm sorry." Lin apologized for almost walking into the man.

In his mid-to-late forties with dark brown hair and a short beard, the man chuckled. "I should also apologize. I was so busy looking into my shop's window display that I didn't notice you approaching."

Lin took a look. The window contained artfully arranged paintings and mirrors and tide clocks and weathervanes. "It looks great. Very inviting. Did you do the window yourself?"

"I did." The man gave Lin an impish smile. "Saves money."

"Have you owned the store long?" Lin asked.

"A few years."

"Have you always worked in retail?"

"Oh, no. I've held many different jobs. I bought the store because it seemed like a good occupation for someone as they grow older. Being a shopkeeper isn't very physically demanding. One must think about such things as they age."

Lin smiled, thinking the man shouldn't be worried about that sort of thing. "You're too young to be concerned about that."

The man's face clouded. "The hand of fate can be quite cruel. My wife died only several years ago."

"I'm very sorry," Lin told the shop owner.

The man sighed. "I lost a good friend not long

after my wife passed away." He shook his head and said thoughtfully, "We think we have all the time in the world, don't we? We think our own personal concerns are the most pressing and important. Sometimes, we don't value enough the ones dear to us until we've lost them."

Lin's eyes widened in surprise. The man's words were very similar in feeling to what she, Viv, and Anton had been talking about only an hour ago. "You're right. I've recently been thinking about the same thing."

"Have you?" The shopkeeper tilted his head and his face looked sad. "Well. It's something to ponder, isn't it? I think it's important to think about how we live our lives, how we treat others. It's important to consider ... before it becomes too late."

A searing sadness came from the man and his words made Lin's heart heavy.

"I must get back to work." The store owner gave Lin a wistful half-smile and disappeared inside his shop.

As Lin continued down the street to complete the errand for Viv, the man's comments repeated in her mind about not making your own wants and needs your only priority and treasuring the people who are important to you.

Lin felt the need to speak to Leonard. She took out her phone and sent a text to him.

I'm sorry I fussed today.

In a few minutes, she received a reply text that made her laugh out loud.

Don't worry about it, Coffin. I'm used to it by now.

13

L in arrived at Anton's house to mow the lawn and weed the flower beds and as soon as she removed her tools from the truck and went around back, the island historian hurried out from his kitchen door to the deck and down to the grass. Nicky greeted Anton by squirming around him and dog-smiling up at the man.

Anton said, "Lin, I was going to call you. I forgot it was mowing day."

Anton could never remember which days Lin came to his home to take care of the landscaping. "I talked to Libby this morning," he said. "She won't be back for another week. I was telling her about your new ghost and the reports of a spirit in the antique

Cape, and surprisingly ... well, I suppose it's not surprising at all considering its Libby, she knew someone who used to rent that house."

He held out a piece of paper to Lin. "Libby said it might be worth getting in touch with her. Here's the information. Libby said she'd talk to the woman so she'd be expecting your call."

Lin took the paper from Anton and looked at the name written on it. *Grace Hand.* "That's great. I'd like to hear about the woman's experiences living in the house." Thinking about the owner of the Cape telling her there was no ghostly presence in the home, Lin said, "There seem to be conflicting opinions about whether a ghost inhabits that house or not."

Anton suggested, "It's possible that the spirit only shows itself to certain people."

"That could be." Lin couldn't put together the separate pieces of information she'd gathered ... the old ghost hadn't shown up for days ... some people claimed there was a ghost in the Cape next to Neil's place, but the owner said there wasn't a ghost at all... when she and Viv were in that house, Lin sensed anger and danger near the back staircase ... and right before leaving the Cape house, the sailor's valentine showed up for several moments on the bookshelf in the living room. Lin took that as a sign that the old ghost was definitely linked to the antique home.

"I need to get back to the library to look up the names I found on the deeds to the old Cape," Lin told Anton. "I've narrowed it down to two people who owned it in the early 1800s and I'm leaning towards G.W. Weeks as being my latest ghost. There must be some other information available about him."

"This ghost is a puzzle," Anton said. "He stays hidden and isn't providing any clues to assist you with understanding what he wants. If I have some time, I'll try and help by doing a little research on G. W. Weeks."

Thanking the historian, Lin started her work on the yard and Nicky and Anton went into the house.

EARLY IN THE EVENING, Lin arrived at Grace Hand's home in Cisco, a sprawling farmhouse on a hill surrounded by several acres of low brush. The area around the house was beautifully landscaped and tended. An older woman with silvery-gray hair sat in a chair on the covered porch and when she saw Lin's truck arrive, she stood and waved, and stepped down to the driveway to meet her.

"You have a lovely home," Lin told the woman after introducing herself.

Grace thanked Lin. "My husband and I do all the gardening. It's quite a lot of work, as you know being a landscaper, but we enjoy doing it and it's very rewarding. We've lived here for over twenty years so we've had a long time to make it what it is."

Grace walked Lin through the gardens providing information about what worked and what didn't and how their ideas about what they wanted the spaces to look like had changed over time.

"Gardens are never static," Lin agreed. "Things are always changing."

Grace brought out some refreshments and she and Lin sat on the porch where a light breeze helped to cool down the hot temperatures of the day.

"Libby tells me you'd like to hear about the time I lived in the old Cape house out by the Polpis Road." Grace poured from a pitcher of lemonade mixed with iced tea.

"I've talked to someone who lived there a few years ago." Lin reported the woman's experiences while renting the house.

"That is very similar to what my husband and I

went through while living in the place." Grace lifted her glass and leaned back in the white, wicker rocker. "We rented the house about twenty-five years ago when we moved to the island to take jobs at the hospital. For many years, we vacationed on-island and loved it so much that when the opportunity came along to move permanently, we jumped on it."

"You rented the house while you looked for something to buy?" Lin asked.

Grace nodded. "We did. We took a six-month lease thinking that would be plenty of time to find our own house." She paused and then said, "It was more than enough time to live in that place."

"You experienced a ghost?"

"We experienced a lot of things. At first, my husband and I didn't mention the odd little things that were going on, thinking we must be mistaken that we'd put something away or locked a door or left a light on. Things slowly escalated though and when they did, Bill confided in me that he worried something was wrong with him." Grace chuckled. "He was so relieved when I told him I experienced all the same things he did and had been worrying about my own sanity. My feelings of relief matched Bill's."

"What were some of the things that went on?" Lin asked.

"Like I said, it started with little things. A cool breeze would come into the room even when there weren't any doors or windows open, a latch would jiggle, a lock wouldn't stay locked, things we put down were moved somewhere else. They were all things you could rationalize were caused by something else, like the house was old so there were drafts, or I must have forgotten that I moved an object, or the lock was worn and sticky and needed to be changed."

"But that's not what it was?" Lin leaned forward.

"It wasn't. Those things were just the beginning. Libby told me you've been inside the house?"

"Only once, for less than an hour," Lin told her.

"You saw the back staircase?" Grace asked.

"I did." The feeling of anger she'd felt near the staircase washed over Lin.

"Bill and I always got the willies near that staircase. We even stopped using it because it made us feel so creepy." Grace gave a shudder. "It was an indistinct feeling, a mix of danger, of harsh feelings, anger, like something dark had happened there."

Lin had experienced the very same impressions.

"Talking with other people about things like this

can be very difficult. Back then, my husband and I brought up the odd happenings with some new friends and they didn't take it well. They looked at us like we were crazy. Someone else we mentioned it to told us there were lots of haunted houses on Nantucket. Bill and I were careful about who we discussed things with, we still are. We work in professional occupations. We don't want to get the reputation that we're unstable or gullible people."

Lin gave the woman a look of understanding. "I've had similar experiences with people. I'm very careful who I share information with." She asked Grace to describe how things in the house had escalated.

"Bill and I began to feel a presence. The cold air would envelope us and we would sense someone was there. The person we sensed always made us feel so very sad." Grace looked down at her hands as she recalled the things that had happened in the house. "Other times we would feel incredible anger around us. It was frightening."

"Did you ever see a spirit?"

"No. Neither one of us saw anything. We did *hear* things though."

Lin leaned forward, eager for Grace to go on.

"We'd be in bed. It would be late at night. We'd

wake up to hear men's voices down the hall. The conversation would become heated. The men would start yelling at one another. Bill would get up and step out of the bedroom and shout at them to stop fighting."

"Would they stop?" Lin's eyes were wide.

"Yes, the voices always stopped as soon as Bill yelled at them." Grace fiddled with a gold band on her finger and rolled her eyes. "Try telling about that experience to your family and friends."

Lin knew first-hand that revealing things about ghosts could only be shared with people who would be accepting of the stories.

"How often did the arguing happen?" Lin asked.

"Three or four times a week." Grace frowned. "After a while, it became commonplace. It was our nightly routine. Go to bed, fall asleep, wake up to the fighting, yell at the men to stop, they stop, go back to sleep. You can see why we were happy we didn't sign a year-long lease."

Lin agreed, "Six months of all that would certainly be long enough."

"There was more." Grace sighed. "Not very often, but on occasion, we'd hear fighting down the hall from our room, near the back staircase. Things would smash against our bedroom door, a candlestick, a book, a paperweight. We assumed it was a ghost or a spirit throwing things in anger. We never felt like it was directed at us personally."

Grace seemed to be thinking about something for several moments, then she said, "Once, we heard what sounded like someone falling down the back stairs. There was the shouting, a thud, a man's scream, and then the falling noises ... and then a terrible piercing wail, like a cry of grief. It was horribly unnerving. The incident happened two nights before we moved out. My husband and I have never forgotten it."

Lin said, "It was lucky that you were about to leave the house. Once was more than enough to hear something like that."

"Yes, it was a huge relief to move away. We'd bought this house. When we moved in, it was such a stark contrast to the rental place. We immediately felt serene, peaceful." Grace smiled. "A month later, we found out I was two months pregnant with our first child. I'm very thankful our children didn't have to live a single day amongst the sadness and grief that permeated that poor Cape house."

14

A t the Whaling Museum in Nantucket town, Lin and Jeff mingled with some people they knew at the evening charity event held to support the island arts community. The building that housed the museum was built around 1846 and was originally a candle factory. The museum was created to display whaling artifacts and to provide information on the history of the whaling industry. In the beautifully restored building, a 46-foot skeleton of a Sperm whale hung suspended from the ceiling in the main exhibition hall. No matter how many times Lin had visited the museum, the sight of the breathtaking skeleton still inspired awe, mixed with a little bit of an eerie feeling from witnessing the whale in such an unnatural location, seemingly swimming through the air.

Wearing a yellow and white sleeveless dress, Lin held Jeff's arm as they walked around greeting friends and acquaintances in the hall of white cloth-covered tables and chairs. The room was decorated with an abundance of floral arrangements and small, glimmering tin lanterns had been placed on the tables and hung here and there along the walls. Waitstaff carried silver trays with drinks and appetizers and several stopped to offer some of the selections to the couple.

Viv, John, and their band had been booked to provide one of the three musical performances of the evening. As the guests enjoyed the drinks, appetizers, and desserts, their band finished the set to rousing applause and Viv, breathless, hurried over to join her cousin.

"Gosh, that went great. I'm so pleased." Viv brushed her bangs back from her forehead and her blue eyes sparkled. "I was so nervous when we started."

"You were terrific." Lin beamed with pride at her cousin's musical ability. "I've never heard you sing better. The crowd really enjoyed the set."

"Now I can relax." With a smile, Viv took a glass

of sparkling champagne from the waiter's silver tray and took a long sip as she surveyed the chattering crowd. When she spotted Jeff and John engrossed in conversation with an older man, she asked, "Who are Jeff and John talking with?"

Lin glanced in the direction that Viv was looking. "He's a developer. Joseph something-or-other. He does a lot of restoration of historic homes. They're all talking about working together."

Viv let out a soft squeal. "John's talked to me about him. His name is Joseph Hickey. He's a multi-millionaire businessman. If they can team up with that guy, it would be very lucrative for them."

A tall, thin, older man in his late sixties wearing a dark suit approached the young women. His blue eyes were light in color and his brown hair, cut close to his head, was mixed with silver. The man's face was kind and he had a gentle manner as he gave Viv a smile and a nod.

"I enjoyed your music," he said softly. "You have a lovely voice."

Viv blushed and extended her hand. "Thank you so much. I'm Vivian Coffin."

"I used to play the violin." The man shook his head slowly with a look of regret on his face. "Oh, how I loved to play. Your performance brought back wonderful memories." He paused for a moment and then said, "I haven't touched my violin for ages."

"Why did you stop?" Viv asked.

"Someone I played with passed away. He and I used to play all sorts of music. My wife would sing. We'd have all the neighbors over for food and song and dancing." The man had a happy, faraway look in his eyes, and then he blinked and gave a slight shrug. "When my friend died, all the joy I used to feel from music disappeared for me."

"I'm very sorry." Viv held the man's eyes and suggested gently, "Maybe now's the time to pick it up again."

The man turned to Lin. "Do you play an instrument?"

Lin said, "I dabbled a little with the piano and guitar, but I'm not a musician by any stretch of the imagination."

"Lin's too modest. She has the talent. She just needs to practice." Viv gave her cousin a soft poke. "Lin has a beautiful singing voice. She's done duets with me on occasion."

"I'd love to hear you sing together." The man smiled warmly. "Will you be singing today?" he asked Lin.

"Oh, no." Lin shook her head with vigor. "I'm not

a performer. Viv and I sing on the deck sometimes in the backyard. I leave the stage to my cousin."

"Cousins." The man seemed thoughtful and then he looked at Lin, his eyes resting on her horseshoe necklace for a second. "You're a Coffin, too."

A shiver of something ran over Lin's skin. "I am."

"Your ancestors were early settlers of the island," he remarked.

Lin said, "I'm descended from Sebastian Coffin and Emily Witchard."

"Oh, I see." The man made eye contact with Lin and a strange feeling rushed through her. "I got the feeling that you are an old soul with deep connections to Nantucket."

Lin was about to ask what he meant by his comment when Viv asked the man, "Are you related to the early settlers?"

"Me? Oh, my, no. My ancestors don't go back that far."

"Were you born on-island?" Viv questioned.

"I was." The man gave a slight chuckle. "A very long time ago."

"What do you do for work?" Viv asked with interest.

"I did all sorts of jobs."

Before Viv could ask any more, two older couples

descended on the three people, apologized for inter-rupting, and then the women of the foursome began babbling at Viv about her band's performance and asking about booking them for a wedding shower while one of the men questioned Lin about being added to her and Leonard's client list for land-scaping services. "I know it's late in the season to be asking, but if there is any way you could squeeze us in, we'd be forever grateful. I've seen your work and there's no better landscaping company on-island."

The prospective customer went on and on about paying more than the going rate in order to retain Lin and Leonard to do his property and when Lin took a moment to glance around for the man she and Viv had been talking with, she noticed that he was gone. Their conversation had left her feeling odd in some vague way and she could barely pay attention to the man who was trying to twist her arm to accept him as a client.

"Let me speak to my partner about fitting you in. Why don't you call our business number and leave your name and contact information and I'll get back to you once we determine if there's a way to fit you in."

The client-to-be grasped Lin's hand in his and shook. "I look forward to speaking with you soon.

Don't forget about us." He, his wife, and their two friends walked away to join another group of people.

"Sheesh," Viv said, commenting on the man's near-desperate attempt to hire Lin and Leonard. "How could you ever say "no" to that guy?"

Lin shook her head while glancing over her cousin's shoulder to look around the event space. "We might have to decline him as a client this year, depending on what sort of landscaping work he wants done. Our client list is very full. We can barely keep up with our work as it is."

Viv noticed that Lin was gazing over her shoulder so she took a peek at the people behind her. "What are you looking at?"

"I'm trying to find the man who was talking to us before those two couples interrupted."

"That man seemed nice, didn't he?" Viv scanned the crowd, but was unable to locate the man. "He seemed kind."

"He gave me a weird feeling." Lin let her eyes trail over the faces of the event attendees.

Viv turned to look Lin in the eye. "Weird? Why? What kind of a feeling did you get?"

"He made me uneasy."

"Why?" Viv studied her cousin's expression. "He

just talked about music and the island and early settlers. Why did that make you feel worried?"

"I don't know." Lin continued to look around the room, her eyes darting from side to side.

"Well," Viv kidded. "The man was solid when I shook his hand, and he spoke to you, and he didn't make you feel cold, so he's a living, breathing man ... not a ghost." When Lin didn't react, Viv narrowed her eyes and her voice shook nervously. "What is it? Do you think there's something wrong with him? Is he a criminal or something? What did you pick up on? Did you sense something? Is he bad? Is he dangerous?"

"I'd like to talk to him some more," Lin said. "That's all."

"I know I asked you this already." Viv pushed at a strand of her hair with trembling fingers and said firmly, "but why do you want to talk to him? What do you feel is wrong with him?"

Lin turned her gaze on Viv. "Nothing's wrong with him. At least, I don't think so."

Viv narrowed her eyes. "Then what's this about him making you feel uneasy?"

"I don't know." Lin's shoulder came up in a slight shrug. "That's why I want to talk to him again."

"Are you linking him to the case? Do you think he might be a descendant of G. W. Weeks?"

Lin's eyes widened as a smile formed over her lips. "Maybe that's it. You're a genius."

"Well, yes, I am," Viv joked. "But what exactly do you feel from him?"

"I just need to talk to him. That's all I know." Lin continued to scan the crowd again.

Viv slipped her arm through her cousin's. "Then let's walk around and try to find the man." Looking over to John and Jeff still huddled in conversation with Joseph Hickey, the developer, she added, "Those three haven't come up for air so John and Jeff won't be looking for us for a while. Let's stroll."

The young women wandered around among the crowd, stopped by the bar, mingled with people they knew, and stood at a high-topped table listening to the last band of the night play a mix of pop, light rock, and folk tunes, all the while looking around for the man they'd chatted with earlier.

"He must have left," Viv sighed. "We've gone around and around in circles with no luck. Our man has flown the coop."

"Too bad." Lin ran her index finger over her horseshoe necklace. "I thought if I could talk to him a little more, I might pick up a clearer impression from him."

"Maybe you'll run into him again." Viv smiled hopefully. "Come on, let's go look for our guys."

The girls found Jeff and John standing off to the side, sipping drinks, in deep conversation with one another.

Jeff's face brightened when he saw Lin walking toward him. "I thought maybe you ran out on me," he said wrapping his girlfriend in a hug.

"That would never happen." When Lin put her arms around Jeff's broad shoulders, she could smell the familiar hint of his aftershave and she was about to lean her head against his shoulder when she spotted her sailor's valentine perched in the center of the table behind them. Lin's heart skipped a beat and her breath caught in her throat.

As Viv walked past to stand next to John, Lin's view was momentarily blocked. A second later, when Viv moved away and the table was visible again, a shiver ran through Lin's body.

The valentine was gone.

15

Stepping back from Jeff's embrace, Lin rubbed her fingers over her forehead.

"Are you okay?" Jeff asked, his hand on Lin's arm and a tone of concern in his voice.

"I...." Lin's vision blurred for a second causing her to reach for Jeff's hand.

"Are you getting a headache?" Jeff placed his free hand on the back of Lin's neck to rub at the muscle tension that had collected there.

"I felt a little unsteady for a second." Lin blew out a long breath as she leaned to her left to take another look at the high table behind them where she thought she'd seen her sailor's valentine. "I thought I...."

John and Viv came up to the couple and John let

out a quiet groan. "Here comes the owner of the antique Cape house. I hope he isn't about to chew me out for not finding a buyer yet."

A tall, stocky man in his late sixties with a head of white hair and a stomach that strained the buttons on his shirt walked up to them and shook John's hand like it was a pump. "John. This is your girlfriend?" He gave Viv a nod. "Great voice, young lady. You should be on the radio." Looking back to John, the man said, "I didn't know you had musical talent. It's a good thing you do. If you don't sell my house soon, maybe you'll need to turn to music full-time." The man threw his head back and chortled at his own joke.

Lin stared at the man. This wasn't the person she'd met at the antique Cape who claimed to be the owner of the house.

John forced a smile. "Mr. Anderson, this is Vivian Coffin, my girlfriend." He then told Viv, "This is Wallace Anderson. I hold the listing for his house."

"Better not hold it too long." Anderson elbowed John in the side. "Any bites on the place?"

"Not as yet." John looked miserable having to admit he didn't have anyone who was interested in the house. To deflect attention away from the topic, John gestured to Jeff and introduced him to Mr.

Anderson and then said, "And you've met Lin previously."

Anderson's forehead wrinkled as he stared at the befuddled-looking, blue-eyed brunette. Confusion had washed over Lin as she tried to recall, without success, ever meeting Wallace Anderson.

Anderson spoke as he reached for Lin's hand. "We have *not* met. Believe me, I'd remember if I'd met this young lady."

It was John's turn to look puzzled. "You met each other at your house the other day. Lin is a landscaper. She's working at the house next door to yours. You and Lin ran into each other and discussed...." John lowered his voice. "You discussed the ghost in your house."

Lin's and Anderson's expressions mirrored one another's look of bewilderment.

"This isn't the man I talked to," Lin told John.

John asked for clarification. "You were at Neil's place working the other day? You said you ran into the owner of the Cape. The Cape next to Neil's house, right?"

"Yes." Lin's voice sounded small and faraway.

John moved his hand around. "This is the owner of that house. Wallace Anderson."

"The man I met said his name was George."

"I never ran into this young lady," Anderson announced.

"You were at Neil's, right?" John asked Lin again.

Thoughts swam in Lin's head as she tried to figure out what was going on. "I was at your house," she told Anderson. "I talked to a man in his thirties. I thought he said he was the owner."

"Whoever you talked to is *not* the owner. Unless, John here, doesn't know the guy made an offer on my place." Anderson gave John the eye.

John flashed Lin a quick look of annoyance. "If someone made an offer, I assure you, Mr. Anderson, that I would know about it and would have presented it to you."

Anderson shifted his attention back to Lin. "What was the mystery man's name?"

"He said his name was George."

"I don't know anyone named George." Anderson shook his head.

Lin asked, "Do you employ a maintenance man for the house?"

"No, I don't," Anderson said before giving John a verbal dig. "But, I might have to if the house doesn't sell soon."

"I hear you have a ghost living in your house," Lin told the man.

"Keep your voice down." Anderson's eyes narrowed as he glanced around at the other event-goers. "Some renters have claimed such a thing. I don't believe in ghosts, but if a potential buyer asks if there is a ghost in the house then the person has to be informed of the foolish rumors."

"Have you ever lived in the Cape?" Lin questioned.

"No, I haven't. The place was purchased strictly as a rental property. The ridiculous ghost stories have made the house a pain in the neck to lease so I put it up for sale." Anderson shot John a dirty look. "Every day it sits there, I'm losing money."

John shifted uncomfortably from foot to foot.

"What do former renters say about a ghost?" Viv spoke up.

Anderson shifted his eyes to Viv. "I don't pay attention to any such nonsense. You'll have to ask the easily-frightened renters about the ghosts they ran into while living in the place. Do they not think an old house makes noises or what?" The tall man sucked in a deep breath and his jowls sagged. "Who knew there were so many people around who believed in spirits? Sheesh. Foolishness."

If Anderson only knew, Lin thought.

"Mr. Anderson, can I get you a drink?" John

maneuvered the man away from his friends. "Why don't we plan to sit down and go over some marketing ideas I have for your place?"

John and Anderson disappeared into the crowd.

"John wants to kill me," Lin moaned as she looked at Viv. "He thinks I'm nuts and that I'm causing problems with his client. We need to tell him about my skill. We can't keep my "ability" from him much longer."

"Oh, jiminy." Viv's cheeks went pink as she groaned. "How on earth do I tell him such a thing?"

"Lin told me and I didn't pass out or anything," Jeff said with a smile. "John will take it just fine."

"Will he?" Viv ran her hand over her face. "John is pragmatic, logical. He has a straightforward mind. He believes in what he can see. I don't know. I just don't know."

"We can't keep it from him forever," Lin said gently.

"I know, I know." Viv looked like she wanted to cry.

Jeff asked, "So what's going on with this George person who told you he owns the antique Cape?"

"I wish I knew." Lin took a seat at the high table and when Jeff and Viv sat down next to her, she told them about seeing the sailor's valentine in the middle of the table to their left. "It was right there." She jabbed the wooden tabletop with her finger. "And then it was gone."

"Oh, no." Viv rested her chin in her hand. "What does it mean?"

"It means there's a clue in this building, at this event," Lin said.

"Is it Anderson?" Viv screwed up her face.

"He could be part of the clue since I found out he's the real owner of the Cape."

"What's this guy, George, up to then?" Jeff asked.

"Did George make you feel cold?" Viv stared at her cousin.

"No ... and he *talked* to me," Lin said. "None of my ghosts have ever talked to me."

"And then there's the guy who said he was the property's maintenance man," Jeff said. "Anderson told us he doesn't employ a maintenance man."

"I've never had a ghost case that has made me feel so flummoxed." Lin sighed in frustration. "The old ghost has only appeared once. I've met two men who have lied to me about working at and owning the Cape. How are they all linked to this mess? What does the ghost want me to find out? Why doesn't he help me?"

Jeff took Lin's hand. "You'll figure it out. You just need more time."

"I'm so, so tired." Lin's upper eyelids drooped.

"Don't give up," Viv said. "Tomorrow afternoon we're going to the library. We'll find some information on the two men you think might be your ghost. We've been so busy that we haven't been able to spend time doing any research. Tomorrow we'll find something that will move the case forward."

A grateful smile played over Lin's face. "When I fall down, you two pick me up."

"That's what we're here for." Viv returned her cousin's smile. "You can't be expected to carry the weight of your "skill" all by yourself." Suddenly, Viv's eyes widened and she sat up straight. "That's it, isn't it?"

"What?" Lin asked.

"I've been wondering and wondering why I can't see ghosts and you can. Why did you inherit our ancestors' skills and I didn't? Why did you get the ability to help the ghosts and I didn't?"

"You figured out why?" Lin asked.

"No, *you* figured it out."

Lin stared blankly at her cousin.

"You fall down and I pick you up. The ability to help ghosts is too much of a burden for one person to bear. My family *skill* is to be the one who helps you. We were born on the same day. We're the same age. We're two peas in a pod. We're a team. That's why you didn't see ghosts again until you moved back to Nantucket ... until you moved back here with me. We're supposed to do this together."

Lin's eyes got all misty. "You're right," she said softly. "I can't do this alone. I need you."

Viv sat in her chair with a triumphant look on her face. "I *didn't* get cheated out of the family skills. I have a role to play, too."

Jeff smiled broadly and squeezed Lin's hand. "That's it. That's why you see ghosts now. They waited to show up because you needed Viv's help."

"Yes." Lin squeezed her boyfriend's hand and looked deeply into his eyes. "And before I could ever tackle all this, I think I needed you, too."

16

L in stood in the dark kitchen with only the light from the living room lamp pooling onto the wood floor. With Nicky sitting quietly at her side and leaning against her leg, she stared at the object on the shelf of the tall hutch. A bit of moonlight played over the sailor's valentine and illuminated the hundreds of tiny, colored shells arranged in the intricate pattern.

On returning from the charity event, Lin showered, made some toast and tea, and sat on the sofa working on a crossword puzzle. Feeling worn out and frustrated over the case, she'd avoided thinking about the valentine or the old ghost and each time she went into the kitchen, she averted her eyes away from the hutch.

When she dozed off for thirty minutes, she dreamed of chasing after bits and pieces of information that swirled in the air and blew just out of reach every time she leaped to grasp them. The dog had curled up next to her on the couch, and when she woke with a start, Lin was comforted and calmed by the rhythmic sound of Nicky's gentle in-and-out breathing. He lifted his head and rested it on her leg, his dark brown eyes looking up at her.

"Why can't I figure this out, Nick?" Lin asked. "I can feel clues darting around me, but I can't grab hold of them and put them in any order."

Despite wanting to avoid the whole thing for a few hours, a strong urge had compelled Lin to get up off the sofa and go to the kitchen to look at the valentine, and she and the dog ended up positioned in front of the old hutch in the dark, quiet room.

Lin had placed the valentine vertically on the shelf so that the shell pattern faced outward and was visible from anywhere in the kitchen, but now it was positioned horizontally on the hutch. Tilting her head as she stared at the object, Lin spoke out loud to the valentine. "When I saw you at the antique Cape the other day and at the Whaling Museum this evening, did you actually leave the house or is what I saw like a hologram or something?"

The look of the shells began to change as if they were being lit from within ... first, the pinkish shells would brighten and fade, then the white ones would illuminate and grow faint, and then the purple shells would light up and dim. The pattern continued and, with wide eyes, Lin shuffled closer to the valentine and reached out to touch it.

As her hand hovered over the octagonal box, her skin warmed from the heat rising off the valentine and she withdrew her hand.

Images, sensations, and snippets of conversations whirled in her brain. Meeting a young man named George at the old Cape house who told her he was the owner ... meeting Wallace Anderson, the real owner of the place, at the evening's charity event ... running into and talking with the maintenance man who told Lin he worked at the Cape ... and Wallace Anderson denying employing a worker for the property.

Lin shook her head as if the movement might help arrange and connect what she knew.

The former renters' words bounced in her mind. Odd things happened in that house the renters told her ... lights would turn on, objects would be moved or flew through the air, locks didn't stay locked, men were heard arguing and yelling in the home, the

Cape's back staircase gave off an air of danger and terrible sadness.

Another thought popped into Lin's mind. Why won't Leonard let me into his house? For a second, the answer seemed to be within reach, but then the particles of the idea spun and swirled away without coalescing. Lin leaned back against the kitchen island and let out a sigh.

When a huge yawn escaped from her mouth, Lin turned and headed for the bedroom. "Come on, Nick. We need to sleep."

The dog let out a woof causing Lin to startle. Her eyes flicked to the valentine and she saw one tiny, white shell lit up so brightly it felt like a searchlight was cutting into her optic nerve. Her eyelids snapped shut and as she whirled away from the light, her hand came up to cover her eyes.

Behind her lids, an image formed of the pile of white scallop shells near the harbor off the Polpis Road that she and Viv discovered while on their bike ride.

Lin's heart raced. There was something about that location. The awful feeling of unease she'd experienced while gazing at those piles of scallop shells flooded through her veins.

Lin looked down at the little dog at her feet. "There's something about those shells, Nick."

The words repeated in her head.

There's something about those shells.

LIN DROVE her truck down the dirt road and pulled it to a stop at the edge of the lane. The early morning sun had only started its climb over the horizon an hour ago, but the air was sticky and held the promise of another scorching hot day.

Barely able to sleep the night before, Lin felt slow and sluggish and wondered how she would drag herself through her work day. The concerns about her stamina faded the closer she got to the end of the road. As her heart began to pound, Nicky looked up at Lin and whined.

"I know, Nick. I feel it, too." Beads of sweat dribbled down Lin's back and the perspiration had little to do with the heat and more to do with the area she was approaching. She stopped at the edge of the huge lot.

The scallop shells spread out before her in one, long, huge white pile. Because the sun was lower in the morning sky, the scene was less bright than the first time she'd seen the dumped shells, but the sense of unease and anxiety was the same, strong and powerful, and it hit her square in the chest.

Nicky whined again and stayed behind his owner, his small face peeking around Lin's legs.

The humid air wrapped itself around the young woman and pressed against her making her lungs feel heavy and tight and she had to force herself to take in slow, deep breaths. The temperature seemed to be rising with each passing minute as Lin stood there staring at the discarded shells. There was an old, long, low building to the left and she could see the bright blue water of the harbor at the far end of the lot.

With tiny drops of sweat beading up above her lip, Lin imagined jumping into the cool ocean to erase her discomfort.

The dog growled low and deep in his throat.

Lin glanced down. "What's making us feel so anxious, Nick?"

Letting her eyes move around the space, Lin tried to determine the cause of the uncomfortable sensation that made her want to run back to the truck and race away down the road to her first client of the day.

Was it the old building? Did something awful

happen on this spot? Was it the sight of the thousands of shells that once housed living creatures strewn over the dusty lot and discarded like garbage?

Muscle tension in her neck clawed its way up into Lin's head causing a pulsing sensation to pound in her temples and her vision to blur and dim. Yanking off the sunglasses that were hooked over the top edge of her tank top, she pushed them over her face to shade her tired eyes.

Nicky rubbed his nose against Lin's bare leg causing his owner to jump.

Letting out a chuckle and squatting down, Lin took the dog's head in her hands and scratched behind both of his ears. "Why don't we get going? I think we've both had enough of being here."

The dog woofed and wagged his little tail as he turned jauntily to head back to the truck.

Before standing up, Lin reached for one of the small scallop shells and rubbed her finger over the smooth surface. With a sigh, she stood and gently tossed it back onto the pile.

With a roaring blast, a wall of icy air pummeled Lin with such force that she stumbled backwards and hit the ground like she'd been run over by a freight train. Prone on the dirt lot, the roar of the wind screamed in her ears and the freezing gale that surrounded her turned her sweat droplets to patches of ice on her skin.

The strangeness of the incident made Lin think she'd been on her back for an hour when in reality it had only been a few seconds before the howling of the wind ceased and the air temperature returned to normal.

Nicky rushed to Lin as she pushed herself up to a seated position and rubbed her hands over her arms. Little grains of dirt clung to her long, brown hair.

"What the heck was that?" The words fell from her mouth even though she had a pretty good idea about what just happened.

Standing on shaky legs and shivering slightly, Lin brushed the dust from her backside and tugged at her shirt to dislodge the dirt that had hit her.

Looking down at the dog, Lin asked, "Did you feel that, too?"

She glanced around at the piles of shells and let out a long sigh. Still rattled by her unexpected crash to the ground, Lin traipsed slowly back to the truck with the dog scurrying along behind.

"There's a ghost here, Nick ... and he or she sure does want me to know about it."

17

I was early evening when Lin and Viv sat at a long, dark oak table reading through reels of fiche that contained stored images of long-ago Nantucket newspapers. Lin pushed back from the fiche reader, stretched her arms over her head, and yawned.

"My eyes are going to fall out of my head," she told her cousin.

"I know," Viv agreed. "We've been here for hours and haven't found a single thing of importance on either one of those guys." The cousins were searching for details and information on G. W. Weeks and E. G. North, the two men who owned the haunted Cape house in the early eighteen-hundreds.

North had lived in the house from 1810-1830 and Weeks was the owner of the home from 1830-1836.

"It's slow going." Lin rubbed at the kinks in her shoulders that had tightened from hunching over the table for so long. "I'm reading every article. I'm afraid if I only scan the documents, then I'll miss something important."

Viv groaned. "This will take us the rest of our lives."

Despite feeling fatigued and disheartened, Lin let out a chuckle at Viv's comment and then clapped her hand over her mouth when an elderly man at the next table gave her a scolding scowl for making noise in the library.

"Why don't we stay for a little while longer," Lin whispered and the two women leaned close to their microfilm readers to carry on the search.

The light-levels were low outside the window when, after more than an hour had passed, Lin lifted her head from the screen and said, "I'm beat and I'm starving. Let's call it a day." She switched off the light on the reading machine and reached down for her bag. When she looked up, Viv still had her face stuck to the microfilm screen.

"Viv?"

Viv held up her index finger and kept reading

what was on the screen. After nearly a minute passed, she pushed back with a smile on her face. "Guess who found something."

Lin's brows went up and her eyes widened. "You did? What is it? Show me."

Viv made a flourishing gesture towards the machine and Lin slid over to read from the screen.

"Oh, how sad." Lin sat back. "G. W. Weeks' wife, Sara, died in childbirth. The baby son died, too."

"Keep reading," Viv encouraged.

Lin paraphrased from the article. "Sara Weeks had studied literature and art and was an accomplished painter. She sang in the church choir. Her father was a prominent Nantucket businessman. Sara worked in her father's office as a bookkeeper."

"Don't stop," Viv said. "Keep going."

Lin leaned close to the microfilm reader and after finishing the obituary, she turned to her cousin with a smile. "It looks like G. W. Weeks is our man."

"Weeks was a sailor." Viv looked proud of her discovery. "He sailed for three years from the ages of eighteen to twenty-one."

"He must have bought the valentine on one of his voyages and brought it back for Sara." Lin talked fast with excitement bubbling up in her voice. "Let's keep reading. Maybe we'll find other articles that mention Weeks."

"What a lovely reward for finding some information," Viv mock-moaned. "I have to stay in this library for a few more hours reading on this awful machine until my eyes cross."

Lin chuckled and turned back to her reader. "When we finish, I'll buy you dinner."

"I'll hold you to that ... and don't you try to weasel out of it." Viv paged through some of the uploaded articles from the long ago newspaper. "And by the way, I'm very hungry. You're going to have a hefty bill."

Lin smiled as she read. "I think I left my wallet at home."

"Ha-ha," Viv deadpanned. "That's a bald-faced lie."

The young women bantered for a few more minutes until they settled into the reading task and after another hour had passed, Viv gave up. "That's it. I'm done. If you want to keep reading, you'll find me asleep over there in the corner on that leather sofa."

"Wait." Lin was about to turn the light off on her machine when something caught her eye and she leaned in to check the story on the screen. "It's his obituary. Here's G. W. Weeks' obituary."

"I was so close to getting out of here," Viv muttered and slumped in her chair. "Let's hear it. It better be good."

Lin said, "It mentions that Weeks was a sailor for several years, but that he didn't want to be gone from home on any more long voyages, so he did odd jobs taking work on a farm for a while, then started his own business doing handyman jobs. Eventually, he ran a store in Nantucket town. Mr. Weeks was musically-inclined and played several instruments. He married his long-time sweetheart, Sara, and they later bought a house a few miles from town. The article mentions that Sara passed away before her husband at the age of thirty-eight."

"How old was Weeks when he died?" Viv asked.

"Seventy-eight."

"He never remarried?"

Lin took another look at the story. "No mention of that, so I guess not."

"Your old ghost is G. W. Weeks," Viv said. "He must have bought the valentine on one of his voyages. He must have given it as a gift to Sara."

Lin gave a nod. "I think so, yes."

Viv looked pensive. "Why does Weeks want you to have the valentine now?"

Lin's face was blank. "I have no idea."

"What does he want you to do with it?"

Lin gave a shrug. "That is still to be determined."

Deep in thought, Viv tapped her chin with her finger. "You got knocked down this morning by the scallop shell piles when that cold wind blew you over."

Lin waited to see where Viv was going with her comments.

"Obviously, a ghost caused that icy gale." Viv shifted her eyes to her cousin. "Clearly, the ghost responsible for knocking you to the ground wanted to get your attention."

"I think that's a good guess."

Viv asked, "Was knocking you down done out of anger?"

"I didn't think of that." Lin's forehead creased in thought.

"Or was it simply done to ensure you knew that a ghost was in the vicinity?"

"I didn't sense any malice when it happened."

"So was it your old ghost, Mr. Weeks, who knocked you down with the icy tsunami?" Viv asked.

"Was he trying to get your attention over something on that lot?"

"I don't know if it was Weeks or not, but whoever it was, the ghost was definitely trying to get my attention." Lin frowned. "And, I've got a butt bruise to prove it."

Viv held up her hand and kidded. "No unnecessary details, please."

"What's the connection?" Lin thought out loud. "Mr. Weeks could have knocked me down in my house. He didn't have to wait until I went to the shell piles. Weeks is trying to tell me something."

Viv said, "He's trying to tell you that there's something you need to be aware of down by the shell piles ... of something on that lot."

Lin nodded. "That's why I felt strange and worried when you and I biked there the other day. I have to figure out what's wrong down there. It's something important."

"At the very least," Viv surmised, "it is something very important to G. W. Weeks."

"It can't be related to his wife," Lin said. "She predeceased her husband."

"She died in childbirth," Viv added. "She wasn't murdered, she didn't disappear. Nobody killed her."

Lin said, "So there's no mystery surrounding Sara Weeks."

"What's the mystery about then?" Viv cocked her head.

"Was or *is* someone doing something illegal down by the shell piles?" Lin questioned. "Whatever it is, it must have something to do with Mr. Weeks."

"We need to go back there." Viv wore a determined expression. "We'll sniff around, see what's going on, look for possible clues."

Lin's shoulders slumped. "What does the area around the shells have to do with the valentine?"

"That's the main question, isn't it?" Viv asked. "We have to find the link between Mr. Weeks, the valentine, and the shell pile lot." She paused. "How are we going to figure it out?"

"Maybe we need to go to the historical museum to do more research." Lin's eyes brightened. "Maybe Anton can help us. We should go talk to him. Pick his brain. He might know something about the area near the shells."

"Good idea." Viv picked up her purse and stood. "Now you owe me a meal."

"Did I agree to that?" Lin teased.

"Yes, you did." Viv slipped her arm through her cousin's. "Let's go." As they left the library and stepped outside into the cooler evening air amidst the people strolling through town, Viv asked, "How's Leonard? Are you two back to normal? Is he still keeping you from going into his house?"

Lin's smile fell away. "We're fine. Things are back to normal. Even though he told me he'd invite me in someday, I don't think it will ever happen. Leonard is a private man. He suffered terribly when his wife died. The loss still haunts him, although he seems to be handling it better than he used to. I know he cares about me. I've given it a lot of thought. I have to be mindful that Leonard's home was Marguerite's home, too, and I don't think he wants anyone intruding into what they had together. I think the house is a symbol to Leonard of their life together."

Suddenly, a wall of icy air enveloped Lin and made her shiver. She turned her head quickly and caught a flash of a dark-haired woman standing on the corner watching her ... and in less than a half-second, the woman faded and disappeared.

18

"Viv." Lin was still staring at the opposite corner of the road. "A woman was standing over there. She was watching me."

Viv looked across the street. "Who was it? Is she gone? Maybe she knows you."

"I didn't recognize her. I only saw her for a second and then she was gone." Lin turned to her cousin and spoke softly. "She was a ghost."

Viv's mouth opened in surprise. "Did you feel cold?"

"Yes." Lin looked up and down the cobble-stone street even though she knew the ghost was gone.

"What did she look like?" Viv asked.

"She was in her mid-thirties, dark shoulder-length hair, slender, pretty." Lin kept looking at the corner of the road.

"She must be related to the old ghost," Viv guessed. "Could she be G. W. Weeks' wife, Sara?"

Lin's eyes had narrowed. "I don't think so."

"What makes you feel that way?" Viv was trying to draw out Lin's impressions.

Lin bit her lower lip. "The way she was dressed. Her clothes looked contemporary. She didn't stand out like she was from another century."

"Okay." Viv's mind was working. "Did you get the feeling she wanted something from you? Did she need help?"

"No." Lin had been surprised to see the woman staring at her. She was sure it was a ghost, but the spirit didn't send her any sensations to pick up on. Ever since she'd moved back to Nantucket, whenever a ghost appeared to her, he or she gave off a strong feeling ... sadness, grief, loss, a longing for something. "She didn't seem to want anything from me. I didn't get any feelings from her at all."

"Are you sure she was looking at you?" Viv questioned. "She might have been looking for or watching someone who was near you."

"Maybe, but I don't think so." Lin's surprise had come from the ghost's deliberate staring. The woman made eye contact with Lin and held her gaze. "She was looking at me, right at me. Her gaze didn't waver. She was staring at me."

The cousins started to walk down the sidewalk.

"Maybe the ghost has heard of you from other ghosts," Viv offered. "Maybe she wanted to see the human who could communicate with spirits."

"I can't communicate with spirits. I can only see them."

"Well, maybe she wanted to have a look at the kooky human who can see ghosts." Viv glanced back over her shoulder. "Forget about her. You claim she doesn't want anything from you, so let it go."

"It makes me uneasy. I've never seen a ghost who doesn't want something from me."

"How about when you were a kid? They didn't want anything from you then, right?" Viv asked.

Lin thought back on her childhood interactions with spirits. "Not really. I guess not."

"Then this must be one of those kinds of ghosts. I don't think it's anything to worry about," Viv encouraged. "You would have felt something if she was out to get you."

A look of horror spread over Lin's face. "Out to get me? I didn't consider that."

"Come on. Stop thinking about it. Let's browse

some stores before we go for dinner. Didn't you say you wanted to look in somewhere?" Viv hoped to distract Lin from the ghost's appearance.

"Yeah." Lin's voice sounded flat. "I wanted to go to the shop next to the place where I bought the valentine. I saw a mirror I liked in the window."

"Great. Let's head that way." Viv picked up the pace to move quickly away from the area where Lin had seen the ghost staring at her. After walking several blocks, they turned onto the side street where the shop Lin was interested in was located.

"Here it is." Lin stopped and pointed to a mirror in the display window. The frame was gold and a sailing ship had been painted on the wood section at the top. "That's the one I like. I thought it would look nice on the living room wall by the front door."

"It's beautiful." Viv looked sideways at Lin. "But, you probably can't afford it."

"Let's go in and see."

The young women entered the high-end shop of paintings, mirrors, sculptures, linens, clocks, and jewelry boxes. Lin approached the clerk and asked about the mirror in the window and when she heard the price, her face blanched. "It's a bit more than I wanted to spend."

With a look of disappointment, Lin sidled up to

Viv who stood at a display table admiring a brass and wood tide clock. "You were right. No way I can afford that mirror."

"Maybe you can find a similar one for less in a different store," Viv said.

Lin overheard one of the customers ask for the owner of the store and when the clerk replied that Mrs. Holder had left for the day, her head snapped up. "I met a man outside on the sidewalk the other evening," she whispered to Viv. "He told me he was the owner of this store."

"Maybe a husband and wife team own the place," Viv suggested.

"Nuh-uh." Lin shook her head. "The man told me his wife died a few years ago."

"He could have remarried."

"I don't think so. He seemed broken up about losing his wife." Lin walked across the space to speak to the clerk. "Could you tell me the name of the store owner? I bumped into him outside on the sidewalk the other night."

The clerk looked confused. "A man? No. Margaret Holder owns the store. She's been the only owner for about twenty years."

Lin's eyebrows scrunched together. "Does Mrs. Holder employ a man to do the window displays?"

The clerk shook her head causing her blond bob to swing around the sides of her chin. "No. A woman from the island does the windows."

"Does a man in his forties with brown hair and a beard work here?" Lin asked.

"No, I'm sorry. No one like that works here at the shop. Maybe you were outside of a different store and confused it with this shop," the clerk said helpfully.

"That could be. Thank you." Lin walked away knowing full well that she was not outside a different shop. She and Viv left the store and stepped into the lamplight where Lin pivoted on the brick sidewalk and faced the display window. "I was standing right here. I almost bumped into the man. We talked next to the window. He said he was the store owner."

"Well, he was lying," Viv decided.

Lin's blue eyes met Viv's. "He wasn't lying. He was sincere."

Viv took a step closer to her cousin. "What did the man say to you?"

"We talked about the store. He told me he lost his wife not long ago." Lin pressed her fingers to her temple. "He said he'd also lost his close friend."

"What else did he say?" Viv tilted her head to the side.

Lin recalled the man's words. "He said we have to treasure our loved ones."

"Did he make you feel cold?"

"No." Lin shook her head. "He was solid. A late-middle-aged guy."

"Are you sure you were outside this store?" Viv asked.

"I'm positive." Lin looked bewildered.

Viv crossed her arms over her chest. "Then he was pretending to own the shop."

"Why would he do that?" Lin questioned, confused by the situation.

Viv said, "He runs into a pretty girl. He wants to impress her so he says he owns the store."

"I don't think so. He didn't seem like that kind of person."

The door near the other side of the display window opened and an older man with silver white hair and leaning on a cane stepped out to the sidewalk.

VIV GESTURED to the door of the shop. "Well, the guy you talked to doesn't own this store. The clerk told you that a woman owns it." She lifted her hand with the palm-side up. "What other explanation is there?"

Lin blew out a long breath of frustration. "I don't know."

The old man tipped his tweed hat to the cousins. "Evening. I apologize for overhearing what you were saying. Are you looking for the shop owner?"

Lin shifted around on the sidewalk to face the man. "I was, yes."

"Mrs. Margaret Holder owns the store." The man's face had deep lines in the skin and dark circles showed under his eyes. "I rent the second floor apartment from her."

"I thought a man owned the place," Lin explained. "I was mistaken."

"It happens." The man gave a kind smile. "Some of the side streets look alike. It's easy to get confused about which store is on which street."

"That must be it," Lin acknowledged.

"I know quite a few of the shop owners here in town," the man said. "Can you describe the man you're looking for? I might be able to help."

Lin told the old man what the person looked like.

"I don't know. I'm sorry. I don't think I can point you in the right direction." The old man's back was slightly stooped. He glanced in the display window.

"I used to own this shop, the whole building, in fact. It was a very long time ago."

"Did you?" Viv asked with interest. "Did you sell the same kinds of merchandise when you owned the place?"

"Some of the same things. It was ages ago. The items that were in demand years ago are not what people are looking for today." He looked up and down the street filled with tourists. "It is still a beautiful town, isn't it? That is one thing that hasn't changed."

"You're still living in the building?" Viv asked.

"That was part of the sale agreement, that I be allowed to live in the apartment as long as I wish. The woman I sold the property to is a very nice person."

"Why did you decide to sell?"

"I was tired. My wife had passed away. My friend was gone. I couldn't keep up with the workload. It was time to let someone else handle the place." The man looked at Viv. "You own the bookstore, don't you?"

Viv smiled, pleased to be recognized. "I do, yes."

"You've done a very nice job with that space."

Viv beamed and thanked the man.

He looked from Viv to Lin. "You are both good

businesswomen." Tipping his hat again, the man wished the girls a goodnight, told them it was pleasant to speak with them, and shuffled away down the street.

Lin and Viv headed for a restaurant down by the docks and when they were a block from the shop they'd just left, Lin stopped in her tracks and stared at her cousin. "How did the man know that I'm a businesswoman, too?"

A shiver of unease ran down Lin's back.

Viv said, "Maybe he's seen you doing land-scaping at the library or working on window boxes at some town businesses."

"He wouldn't know I was the one who owned the business."

Viv gave a shrug. "Maybe he guessed."

Lin knew that wasn't the case. Something was off ... she could feel it.

19

J ust as Lin opened the front door of her cottage to leave for work, Anton Wilson pulled his convertible to a stop in front of her house and jumped out. Nicky stood at Lin's feet, wagged his little tail, and let out a woof to greet the historian.

"What's up?" Lin asked, surprised to see Anton so early in the morning.

"Libby called me." The man was out of breath. "She found someone else you need to speak to. Libby was discussing your case with some people she knows and one of them told her about a woman who used to rent the old Cape house." Anton removed a fresh white handkerchief from his back pocket and dabbed at the perspiration on his brow. "It's too hot for me. Give me a cool, dark library research room any time."

"The woman experienced a ghost?" Lin asked trying to get Anton back on track.

"You need to talk to her. Libby doesn't know the woman personally, she's a friend of a friend." Anton handed Lin a small piece of paper. "Here's her name and number. You have to go now. She's at the docks. She's taking the early ferry back to the mainland."

"She doesn't live here anymore?"

"She and her family live in Boston. She was only here for a short visit." Anton took Lin's arm. "Go now or you'll miss her. Call and let her know you're coming. Tell her Libby's friend, Phyllis Duncan, told you to call."

"But, I have to get to work," Lin protested.

"I'm your first client of the day," Anton said. "I'll give you today off."

Lin's eyes widened. "You usually don't know when I'm scheduled to work in your yard."

"I checked the calendar," Anton said. "I haven't seen you for a few days. I figured you could shuffle the clients around, if need be. Libby said this woman has good information. Go on, now. Shall I take the dog with me?"

"No, he can come to the docks with me. It will save time if I don't have to come get him at your house later." Lin let Nicky in on the passenger side and then climbed inside her truck. As she pulled away, she called a "thank you" to Anton who stood next to his red convertible and watched them go.

LIN MET the woman on Straight Wharf near the ferry office. "I'm Donna Bigley. The ferry doesn't leave for forty-five minutes. There's a bench in the shade over that way. Why don't we go sit?"

When they were settled, Donna leaned forward and gave Nicky a pat. "What a nice dog." The woman was in her late forties, had short brown hair, and was wearing a sleeveless summer dress. "Since you mentioned Phyllis, I know what you probably want to talk to me about." She didn't look happy about it.

"My friend, Libby, knows Phyllis. She said it would be helpful if I could speak with you."

"If you don't mind, I'm not going to ask why it would be helpful to you." Donna looked down the brick walkways. Even though it was early, people were strolling along past the restaurants and stores, some carrying take-out cups of coffee, some holding the hands of small children. In front of them to the left, a sailboat bobbed gently at its mooring.

Donna said, "Things that went on in the old house can't be explained, at least not in a way I'm able to understand. I've talked to Phyllis about our experiences and she's been a help, but whenever she explains one thing, I end up with fifty more questions. It isn't easy for me to say, but I've accepted that there are things in the world that ... well ... that I didn't think were possible." The woman let out a long, slow breath. "I don't talk about this with people, not even with my husband, but on occasion, Phyllis asks me to do a favor and I do it."

Lin nodded. "I appreciate it."

"What can I tell you?" Donna said with resignation.

"When did you rent the Cape house?"

"It was about six years ago. We rented for a year. Our boys were four and two."

"What were your experiences?"

"It wasn't really my experience in the house that you want to hear about. My husband and I didn't see or hear anything out of the ordinary. Well, not until the day we moved out." Donna swallowed. "It was our older boy, Kyle. He had ... he interacted with ...

he said a man talked to him while we lived there. Kyle called him his friend."

"The friend was in the house?" Lin asked.

"In the house, in the yard. Kyle talked about the man in a nonchalant way. I thought it was some imaginary pal that he'd made up."

"It wasn't?"

Donna shook her head.

"What did Kyle say about the man?"

"Kyle said the man stood at the end of his bed sometimes. Kyle was never afraid of him. The man seemed to comfort him. Sometimes, Kyle said the man would watch him play or he'd warn Kyle to be careful." Donna smiled. "A few times, the man told my son that his mother wouldn't want him doing whatever it was Kyle was doing. Sometimes, they'd just sit and talk about things."

Lin sat up. "The ghost talked to Kyle?"

Donna winced at the word "ghost." "Kyle told me he talked to the man a lot, but the man didn't say words with his mouth like people do. He talked to my son, but his words were heard in Kyle's *mind*."

"So some kind of mental communication?"

"I guess so." Donna fiddled with her wedding band. "My husband wanted to buy a couple of kayaks. He was gung-ho that the boys learn outdoor skills. One day, Kyle told me that his friend said that the family should *not* own kayaks. The man said it was fine to learn to sail, canoe, kayak, and swim, but that *we* should never *own* any kayaks."

"Did Kyle say why not?" Lin asked.

Donna's facial muscles stiffened. "The man told Kyle that if we bought kayaks, then his little brother would be in an accident and he would drown."

Lin's breath caught in her throat. "Wow," she said softly.

"Yeah. Needless to say we never bought kayaks." Donna shifted on the bench to face Lin and didn't say anything for a few moments, then she asked with a soft voice, "Do you talk to ghosts?"

Lin was surprised at the question. "I ... I talk to them, but they never talk to me."

"Do they talk to you mentally like this man talked to Kyle?"

"No. They never say anything to me, not with a voice and not mentally either."

"You can see them though?" Donna asked.

Lin nodded. "The air around me gets cold when someone shows up and then I see them."

"What do they look like? Do they look like normal people?"

"They look sort of see-through or translucent, but other than that, they look normal," Lin told the woman. "Have you asked Kyle what he sees?"

Donna gave a hard shake of her head. "I never asked him. It's dumb, I know, but I hoped it would go away if we didn't talk about it. I never knew how to handle it."

"Does Kyle still see the ghost-man?"

"No. When we moved out of the house, Kyle never mentioned the man again."

"You said something happened on the day you moved out?" Lin asked.

Donna looked away from Lin. "I was in the kitchen, fiddling with boxes. I looked out of the kitchen window."

Lin could see the muscle in Donna's jaw tighten.

"There was a man standing outside looking in through the window at me. He looked me in the eye. The man was wearing a tweed cap. He took it off and placed it over his heart." Donna's eyes got misty. "He nodded to me with a kind smile, and then he disappeared."

"Did you tell Kyle you saw him?"

"No." The word was barely loud enough to hear. Donna swiped at a tear that had escaped from her eye. "I don't know why I didn't."

"Did seeing the man scare you?"

"No, it didn't. It was ... almost ... comforting." Donna made eye contact with Lin. "The boys went to get ice cream. When they come back, will you talk to Kyle? Tell him you can see what he used to see."

Lin asked, "Why do you want me to do that?"

Donna's throat was tight. "I don't want him to think he's odd. I don't want him to think he's the only one. Will you tell him you're like him? Please?"

Lin knew that feeling. To feel alone, different, apart from others. "Yes."

Donna was looking over Lin's shoulder. "There they are." She waved her two sons over and introduced them to Lin, and then she stood up. "Joey, come with me to pick up the ferry tickets. Kyle, talk to Lin for a minute and then meet us in the line." Donna and Joey hurried away across the pedestrian walkway to the ferry terminal.

Ten-year-old Kyle looked shyly at Lin. He was tall for his age, with shiny blond hair, and a slim build. The boy leaned down and let Nicky lick some ice cream from his finger. "Nice dog."

Lin said gently, "When you were little, you used to have a friend? A man that was kind to you. He talked to you, but other people couldn't see or hear him?"

Kyle's eyes widened and the corners of his mouth turned up a little. "Did you have a friend?"

"Not exactly like you did, but I could see things that other people couldn't."

"Can you still?"

"Yes."

A grin spread over the boy's face.

"You're not alone," Lin said. "Other people are like us. If you ever want to talk to me about it, tell your mom to get in touch with me. Okay?"

Kyle nodded happily.

"Do you want to ask me anything before your mom and brother come out of the terminal?"

Kyle shook his head. "But, I need to tell you something." He saw his mom coming out of the ferry office and waving him over to join her, so he spoke quickly. "I'm supposed to give you a message."

Lin's jaw dropped.

The boy whispered, "Dig in the shells."

Lin's heart skipped a beat. "Who is the message from?"

"My friend." The boy smiled at Lin and then he ran over to his mother. As the family joined the line of passengers for the ferry, Kyle turned and waved goodbye.

Lin, her head spinning and feeling almost dizzy

from hearing the message, raised her hand to return the wave, smiled at the boy, and nodded.

20

I t was late afternoon when Lin and Jeff met at the Francis Street Beach off Washington Street to rent stand-up paddleboards and practice with them in the calm waters of the small harbor close to town. They'd considered buying two of the boards so they could take them to different beaches and inlets on the island, but wanted to try them a few times to be sure it was something they enjoyed. The afternoon's adventure was only the second time they'd given the activity a try and it was clear to anyone watching that Lin and Jeff were not experts.

Feeling slightly shaky at first, the two quickly settled into a rhythm of balancing themselves while paddling and they moved side by side around the harbor admiring the boats and chatting.

"I didn't work at Neil's house today," Jeff said. "I helped Kurt out at a renovation project he's running in Shimmo. They've fallen behind and he asked if I could lend a hand for a couple of days until they get back on track." Kurt ran a building and renovation company on the island and Jeff had worked closely with him on many projects.

"How did it go?" Lin dipped her paddle into the ocean and pushed it back to slide the board over the water.

"One day working on that house project would be plenty for me," Jeff said. "I'm not looking forward to going back there."

In the past, Jeff had always enjoyed working as part of Kurt's crew so Lin was surprised to hear that he didn't like this particular job. "Why don't you want to return?"

"Kurt hired a couple of new guys. He isn't happy with them so far. Part of the reason he asked me to work a couple of days was to get a second opinion about the new workers." Jeff shook his head. "I'm sorry to admit that I don't have good words to say."

Lin asked what the problem was with the men.

"I think one of the guys could be mentored, but

the other one, Les is his name, I just don't know. He doesn't seem to have a work ethic. He acts foolish."

Lin and Jeff maneuvered their boards to the left of an oncoming kayak to avoid the possibility of a collision. The paddler seemed unable to move the small boat in the direction he wanted to go.

"Does he do good work?" Lin questioned.

"What Les manages to do looks nicely done." Jeff paddled around two sailboats at their moorings. "But he takes a break every fifteen minutes. Kurt came by for a couple of hours and Les actually worked. He's like a split personality, when Kurt is there, he acts mature and hardworking. When Kurt isn't around, Les goofs off, makes off-color jokes, isn't careful with the work, acts silly and childish, doesn't try to do his best."

"It sounds like there are different aged men living in his body," Lin observed. "A late teen and a forty-year-old man."

"That's exactly what it's like. It's weird."

"Good thing you declined the project in favor of doing Neil's place," Lin said.

"That's for sure. With Les, I never know who is going to show up from minute to minute, the teenager or the forty-year-old." Jeff couldn't help but chuckle. "Maybe tomorrow, there will be a new person inhabiting Les' body."

A shiver of something ran over Lin's skin and she tried to focus on what might have caused the sensation, but was unsuccessful.

"One more day and I can get back to Neil's house," Jeff said with a tone of relief. "I really regret doing this."

Again, something picked at Lin and caused a flurry of unease to flicker through her veins.

As the time passed, the paddlers became more comfortable and began to move with grace and ease traveling past the edge of the sandy beach and then stroking back out into the deeper water of the harbor. Gulls flew overhead, colorful canoes and kayaks dotted the bright blue of the sea, and several smaller boats left the cove for an evening sail.

"What's new with your case?" Jeff asked.

Lin glanced around to see if anyone was paddling or boating nearby. "I was going to tell you after we returned the boards. Something unusual happened." She reported to Jeff about talking with the woman who once rented the old Cape with her family. "Her son, Kyle, had a friend ... who was a ghost. Kyle could see the ghost and could communicate with him. He was an older man."

Jeff almost lost his balance and had to contort his body to keep from falling into the harbor. "That's amazing. How old is the boy?"

"He's about ten now," Lin said. "He was four when he met the ghost. Kyle's mother thinks that the boy hasn't been interacting with the ghost since they've moved from the rental house."

"But?" Jeff asked.

"But, it seems Kyle continues to be in contact with the ghost."

"The boy told you this?"

"Not in so many words." Lin dipped her paddle and turned her head to look at her boyfriend. "The boy had a message for me from his ghost."

Jeff stopped paddling and stared at Lin. "How?"

"I think the boy's ghost is my new ghost. I think it's G. W. Weeks. Weeks must have known that I would talk to the boy so he asked him to give me a message."

"And what was the message?"

When Lin told him, she watched the emotions flicker over Jeff's face, disbelief, fear, worry, and then acceptance.

"It's all so hard to fathom," Jeff said as he took in a deep breath. "It makes me want to ask a million questions."

"Me, too." Lin held Jeff's eyes. "Except there really isn't anyone to ask for answers. Libby is helpful, but so many things are a mystery to her as well."

Jeff gave an empathetic nod.

"I told the boy that I could see ghosts, too, and that there were other people like us. It seemed to make him happy." Lin paddled her board closer to Jeff's. "I know what it feels like to know something that others might misinterpret. I know what it feels like to have to keep a secret from people. It's isolating. It can make you feel very lonely."

Bits and pieces of images, thoughts, and words swirled around in Lin's mind and for a second, it seemed that she might grasp on to something important, but as often happened, whatever it was, it turned to dust and blew away.

Jeff suggested they turn around and return the paddleboards and when Lin made the about-face, she took a look at the land bending and jutting out into the harbor and she knew the mounds of scallop shells were down the coast, close to the water, only about a mile away.

A sudden gust of wind blew around Lin and the breeze carried a heavy sensation of aloneness that was like smoky tendrils touching her skin, making her shudder.

When they reached the shore, Lin and Jeff hauled the boards out of the water and returned them to the rental place.

"Why don't we get carry-out food in town and bring it back to your house," Jeff suggested. "It's a nice evening. We can eat out on the deck."

Deciding to pick up meals from the barbecue restaurant to take home, they walked back to town, hand-in-hand, in silence, each one lost in their own thoughts.

Snippets of their conversation kept replaying in Lin's mind like there was something they'd said while paddle-boarding that might be helpful to the case of the old ghost and the sailor's valentine.

The ghost was clearly pointing Lin to the scallop shells, but what did the valentine have to do with any of it? Why doesn't the ghost show up and help point me in the right direction? Why can that young boy see *and* hear the ghost? Being able to communicate with spirits would make things so much easier. Lin let out a little sigh.

"I'm dreading going back to the Shimmo house renovation tomorrow," Jeff admitted. "That guy, Les, is so hard to work with, the way his behavior swerves from childish to more mature is kind of unnerving.

You never know which part of him is going to show up next."

Lin turned her head quickly and looked at Jeff with wide eyes.

Somehow she knew that what he'd just said could be applied to her ghost ... but how? And why?

21

L in, Viv, and Anton sat around his long, wooden, kitchen table. Queenie and Nicky rested in the easy chair that stood next to the fireplace hearth. Lin was reporting what had happened when she met with Donna Bigley and her son down by the ferry dock.

"And after he gave me the message, he ran over to join his mom and brother in line."

Viv and Anton stared at Lin open-mouthed.

"That was my reaction, too. I was so surprised that I didn't say anything for a long while. He told me his friend asked him to give me the message."

"Incredible," Viv said softly. "The ghost must still talk to that boy."

"The boy's ghost has to be the old ghost who

visited you," Anton said to Lin. "The boy's friend must be G. W. Weeks. Did the boy refer to the ghost by name?"

"No, he always called him 'my friend'."

Viv said, "So when you told Kyle you could see ghosts, he knew you were the one he was supposed to give the message to."

"How very interesting." Anton pushed his black framed eyeglasses up to the bridge of his nose. "You and Kyle can both see ghosts, but Kyle can also hear their words."

"Why doesn't the ghost just tell Kyle what he wants?" Viv asked and turned to Lin. "Why bother with you at all?"

Lin leveled her eyes at her cousin. "Thanks a lot."

"No, no. I'm not belittling what you can do." Viv hadn't meant to insult Lin. "I just mean if the boy can hear the ghost, why doesn't the ghost just straight-up tell him what he wants?"

"It could be the ghost doesn't want to burden the young boy with difficult things," Anton said thoughtfully. "Perhaps, a gruesome discovery awaits under the shells and the ghost needs an adult to deal with that."

Queenie lifted her gray head and trilled.

"That makes sense," Lin said. "The boy is too

young to make a sad discovery. I'm not expecting to find anything good under the shells. I'll bet there's no buried treasure hidden under there."

Viv said, "We need to find out what *is* buried there so the authorities will handle the digging."

Bits of information spun around in Lin's head. "Let's start with the assumption that it's a person who's buried in the shells. We can look for articles reporting on a murder or a missing person from the time period in question."

"If it's a person buried there," Viv said, "then G. W. Weeks must have known him and that's why he appeared to you for help."

Something pinged Lin's senses, but whatever it was evaporated before she could grasp it. She said with hesitation, "I wonder if Weeks killed whoever is buried in the shells."

"Oh," Viv muttered. "I didn't expect that the old ghost might be a killer."

"Shall we get to work?" Anton asked sliding his laptop over the table to bring it closer to him. "I've recently been given access to the library's online databases for research purposes. I'll scan the records and newspapers while the two of you start going through my books and articles." Tapping on the keyboard, he said, "We're in for a long evening."

After two hours of searching, Anton heated up a stew he'd made the night before and served it in blue and white bowls with some garlic bread and red wine. "The limit is one glass each," the historian tutted when Viv reached for the bottle to top off her glass. "We can't take the chance of clouding our minds."

Viv ignored the man. "This research work is clouding my mind. The wine will get me through it."

The cat and dog received plates of cut-up stew meat and everyone gobbled their meals with the humans enjoying the food and the break from the tedious effort of looking for a needle in a haystack.

Returning to their task after cleaning up the dishes, Viv moaned, "Can't we go to the police and tell them we suspect someone or something is buried under the scallop shells. Wouldn't that be enough to get them involved?"

Lin and Anton lifted their heads and looked at Viv.

"What would we say?" Lin folded her hands on the table. "A ghost told us to dig in the shells?"

"The authorities don't have the workforce or the funds to go off investigating without some evidence or probable cause," Anton explained. "People would be sending law enforcement out on endless wild goose chases. Nothing would get done. It would be misuse of police time and money. Even finding the name of a missing person somehow associated with G. W. Weeks won't be enough to have them look into it."

"Then why are we doing this?" Viv pouted.

Anton said, "Because it will be a piece of evidence gathered to advance our investigation. Tonight won't be the end of our work, it will only be the start. In fact, we may never get enough information to convince the police to dig."

"Could we dig ourselves?" Viv asked.

"That would be a monumental task," Anton said shaking his head. "We would also need the permission of the lot's owner to access the shell piles."

Lin added, "The owner would probably think we were crazy if we proposed a digging expedition in the discarded shells."

Anton gestured to his laptop and the books scattered over the table. "Let's see what we can find and then we'll plan our next step."

With a reluctant sigh, Viv followed Lin's and Anton's lead and returned to scanning through the book in front of her.

It was approaching midnight when Viv threw in the towel and she and Queenie headed home. Nicky was on his back snoring in the chair when Anton suggested that they give up for the evening.

As soon as he'd made the suggestion, Lin sat up and nearly shouted, "Look here!" She pointed to a page in the book collection of old Nantucket newspapers.

Nicky startled, jumped to his feet blinking, and let out a bark as Anton rushed from his seat to look over Lin's shoulder.

"Here." Lin ran her finger down the short article. "The story from 1835 reports a man who has gone missing. His wife went to the police after her husband did not return home from visiting a friend the previous evening. She contacted the friend and the man told her that he and her husband had enjoyed some dinner and whiskey, had a chat, and then the man left to walk home about 11pm. He had not heard from him since that time."

Lin looked up. "The friend of the missing man was G. W. Weeks."

Anton's face was serious. "This is part of what your ghost wants us to find. What was the missing man's name?"

"Robert Ward." The name bounced around in Lin's head and sent a chill down both of her arms.

"What happened to him?" her voice was almost a whisper. "What happened to Mr. Weeks' friend?"

"Flip to the next pages," Anton suggested. "See if there are any follow-up stories."

Lin turned a few pages. "Here it is. Here's another article." Lin read and paraphrased the information. "Robert Ward, missing since leaving the home of his friend, G. W. Weeks, is assumed dead by Nantucket Police. Ward disappeared after spending an evening at the home of Mr. Weeks. Police believe that Ward, after having several drinks, may have lost his way in the darkness and fell into a nearby marsh where he drowned. The search for the man has been suspended."

"If Mr. Ward fell into the marsh and drowned," Anton asked, "how did he end up buried under the scallop shells?"

"A very good question," Lin said. "I'd bet that Mr. Ward never fell into any marsh. I'd put my money on murder."

Anton asked, "If someone murdered the man, how did G. W. Weeks know where the body was buried? Was he a witness?"

Lin made eye contact with Anton and said the words she hoped were not true. "Maybe Weeks killed Ward himself." Her heart clenched and a moment of dizziness engulfed her. Could her ghost be a murderer? Did G. W. Weeks kill his friend? Are guilt and grief tormenting his soul and keeping him from crossing over? Is that why he came to Lin for help?

Lin bolted out of her chair. "I need to go home. I need to see the valentine."

"I'll drive you." Anton hurried to the sideboard to get his keys.

Looking off across the cozy kitchen focusing on nothing, Lin imagined the pieces of clues and information that had been gathered over the past several days arranging themselves like the letters in a sentence coming together to form a message. Although she couldn't yet read the words, she had an idea of what they might be telling her.

"Oh," was all Lin said, but the expression on her face caused Anton to halt in place.

"What is it?" The historian rushed to Lin's side. "Do you need to sit down?"

"Yes." But instead of taking a seat, Lin began to pace back and forth across the kitchen. "Anton, I don't understand it, but there's something about the people I've run into recently."

"I don't know what you mean." Anton squinted

at the young woman trying to make sense of her words.

"The people I've talked to recently. My interactions with those people are similar to something Jeff said to me yesterday about a guy he'd been working with on a project. He told me he never knew which part of who the guy was would show up." Lin ran her hand over her hair with a look of bewilderment on her face. "Those people. They're clues. I know it."

Anton stared at Lin and shook his head in confusion. "I don't understand a word of what you're saying."

Lin stepped close and put her hand on Anton's arm. "Can you pull up G. W. Weeks' obituary from the online database?"

"Yes," Anton said.

"Hurry," Lin urged. "Before my idea slips from my grasp."

22

Anton's fingers flew over the keyboard. "Here it is." He pushed his chair to the left so Lin could squeeze in beside him.

She read from the screen. "Native Nantucket resident, George W. Weeks, passed away at the age of seventy-eight. A sailor for several years, Weeks went on to work as a farmhand, a handyman, and then owned and operated a store in Nantucket town. Mr. Weeks was a musician who played several instruments. He and his wife, Sara, purchased a house a few miles from town. Sara Weeks and the couple's infant son predeceased Weeks. Mr. Weeks lived for several years, until his death, in the apartment above the store he had previously owned in Nantucket town."

"You read Mr. Weeks' obituary before," Anton pointed out. "Why did you want to see it again?"

"Because suddenly everything clicked."

"You know what happened to Weeks' friend, Robert Ward?"

"No, but I know that Weeks has been trying to tell me things and I completely missed them."

"What things?" Anton asked.

"G. W. Weeks has been making appearances here and there all over town. He's shown up more than a few times and talked to me."

"The ghost talked to you?" Anton's eyebrows shot up. "This is something new. A ghost has never talked to you before."

"He wasn't actually a ghost when he talked to me." Lin scratched her head. "I don't understand it, really, but he's shown up as himself from different times of his life and has tried to pass me clues each time we talked."

"I don't understand," Anton said.

"The first time I saw him Weeks a young man. I saw him pass by my living room window. Viv went to answer the door, but no one was there. Then one night, I saw a young man leading a horse up my street. The man was Weeks when he was young and working as a farmhand."

Anton frowned in confusion.

"Keep listening," Lin encouraged. "Then I met a man named George who was working at the antique Cape house. He told me he was the caretaker. I should have figured it out because I found out later there was no caretaker working there. Later, I met a man who told me he was the owner of the house … it was Weeks, although I didn't know it at the time. Weeks was the owner of the house once, but that was nearly two hundred years ago." Lin turned to face Anton. "You see, Weeks kept running into me from different periods of his life … the young sailor returned from a voyage, a farmhand, a handyman, the owner of the Cape house. Each time we talked, he offered me some clues, but I was too dense to pick up on what was going on."

"When he showed up, was he a ghost?" Anton asked.

"No. I never felt cold when I talked to him. He was solid, not a ghost. It's like he traveled to see me on a river of time. He wasn't dead those times he talked to me."

Anton seemed to pale at Lin's explanation.

"I don't understand it, either, but it's the only way I can make sense of what he's been doing." Lin rubbed at the tension in her neck. "I saw him in town a couple of times. He told me he owned the store we were standing in front of. He told me his wife had passed away and he said he'd lost a dear friend, someone who played music with him, someone he missed terribly."

"His friend, Robert Ward," Anton said.

"He talked about his friend in such a caring way," Lin recalled. "How could Weeks have killed his friend?"

"A fight between them? Did the friend wrong Weeks in some way?" Anton asked. "Robert Ward must be buried under the shells. That's why Weeks asked the young boy to tell you to dig under the shells."

"The last time I saw Weeks," Lin said, "I was with Viv in town. Weeks was an old man. He walked with a cane. He told us he lived in the second floor apartment above the store he used to own. Weeks knew Viv and I owned businesses."

"Mr. Weeks worked hard to pass clues to you," Anton said, amazed by the experiences.

"Yes, he did," Lin said wistfully and then sighed. "I don't believe I'll see Mr. Weeks again. Not as a living man anyway. I think he's given me all the information that he can. Now I have to figure out how to find what's buried under the scallop shells."

"Most likely it's Robert Ward," Anton said.

The weight of the task pressed heavily on Lin. "Weeks also wants me to find out something else. He wants me to know how and why Robert Ward died and how he ended up buried under a pile of discarded scallop shells. I'm afraid my ghost is a murderer."

Lin slumped in the chair. It was after 1am. "Would you drive me home, Anton? I'm exhausted."

Anton picked up the keys from the table and drove the tired young woman and her dog back to her cottage at the outskirts of town.

LIN, Jeff, and Viv stood at the edge of the lot in front of the huge piles of white shells. The night before, Lin had brought her cousin and boyfriend up to speed on the latest information.

"Every time Weeks showed up, he was alive?" Viv shook her head. "He visited you from different times in his life? How did he do that?"

Lin gave Viv a look. "I don't know how any of this works. I don't know how ghosts show up and I sure don't know how Weeks managed to appear from different time periods of his life. All I know is they do and he did."

"For Pete's sake." Viv shook her head slowly. "I just got used to ghosts and now this new twist. Is anything else going to happen that I don't understand?"

Jeff and Lin said simultaneously, "Probably."

The hot sun beat down on them while the three stared at the mounds of shells.

"So, what do you think?" Lin asked.

"I think we could get some heavy equipment from my buddy," Jeff said. "But isn't digging up a body delicate work?"

"It is on TV crime shows," Viv said. "You can't just take a big digging machine and plow into the shell piles. That would break the skeleton apart. You need a crime scene investigator. You need a medical examiner."

"We don't have any of those." Lin stood with her arms hanging down by her sides. "Any ideas?"

"We could get shovels and screens and dig ourselves," Viv said.

"That could take quite a while," Jeff warned. "And we really don't know what we're doing. Besides that, we need to get permission to do any digging. That could be difficult. What will we say? A man from two hundred years ago visited Lin and gave her clues about someone buried here? We could also bring up the ten-year-old boy who gave Lin a message from a ghost."

"I think that would work," Viv chuckled.

Despite the smile on her face, Lin forced her tone to be serious. "I need to figure out a way to do this."

Jeff put his arm around Lin's shoulders. "The body under the shells has been here for almost two hundred years. Waiting another week or so to give us time to figure out what to do won't make any difference."

Lin gave a reluctant nod and they started to walk back to their vehicles. Half-way to her truck, a cold whoosh of air blew over Lin's skin and she turned slowly to look at the shell piles.

At the top of the highest mound, Lin's sailor's valentine balanced on the shells. A bright light glowed from the object and the tiny patterned shells under the glass of the wooden box began to light up in an organized, sequential manner as if someone had connected the valentine to electric circuits that controlled the brightening and dimming of the colored shells. In a moment, the valentine faded and was gone.

Lin's phone buzzed in her pocket and she removed it to read the incoming text. It was from Leonard.

Where are you, Coffin? I thought you were picking me up to go take a look at that new project.

Lin tapped out a return text as she and Nicky hurried to the truck.

I got held up. I'm on my way.

Lin placed her phone on the center console and was about to turn the key in the ignition, when she glanced down at it.

Leonard.

Something floated on the air. Something important.

23

L in pulled into the driveway of Leonard's carefully tended home and cut the engine. With his tail wiggling back and forth, Nicky had his paws on the dashboard looking eagerly out the front window waiting for the man to emerge from the house.

Lin didn't know why she felt so antsy, but her nerves fired out of sync making her want to get out of the truck and go for a run to rid herself of the unsettling excess energy. She absent-mindedly tapped her finger on the steering wheel thinking that her agitation came from the problem of how to dig at the scallop shells.

After five minutes had passed without Leonard

coming out of the house, the dog looked at Lin and whined.

"I know," she said. "He was in such a hurry and now he's dawdling." Lin lightly tapped the horn to alert Leonard to their arrival.

"What's he doing in there?" Lin's voice held a tone of irritation.

When Nicky barked, a zap of adrenaline pulsed through Lin's veins and she pushed the driver's side door open and strode to the front of the house with the dog running ahead of her. When she pushed on the doorbell button, Lin heard the tinkling chimes sound inside the house. Just as she raised her hand to knock, Leonard opened the door, his face looking drawn and tight.

"What's wrong with you?" Lin asked concerned at the man's pale appearance. "Are you feeling sick?"

"No." Leonard stood unmoving on the other side of the screen door.

A few moments of awkwardness lingered between them until Lin asked, "Are you ready to go?"

Nicky whined, not understanding why Leonard wouldn't come out.

"I forgot my lunchbox in the kitchen." The man didn't move to go and retrieve it.

"Okay," Lin said through the screen. She waited and then said, "Are you going to go get it?"

Without saying a word, Leonard lifted his hand and opened the door so that Lin and Nicky could enter.

Lin's eyes went wide and her mouth opened. The dog looked up at his owner, unsure of what to do.

Leonard gestured for them to come inside.

Gingerly, Lin stepped over the threshold into the small entryway and Nicky followed with hesitation.

The entry opened into a large living room with cream-colored walls, a fireplace on the far wall, a model of a sailing ship on the mantle, a patterned rug of soft blues, rose and cream on the floor, and a sofa and chairs in shades of muted blues and white placed in a grouping near the fireplace. Light flooded into the room through big windows and a few vases of fresh flowers had been set on the coffee table and side tables. The space was elegant, welcoming, and cozy all at the same time.

"This is the living room," Leonard muttered, his voice sounding tense.

"It's beautiful." Lin smiled softly, shocked and surprised that she'd been invited in.

"The dining room is over there." Leonard pointed to the room open to the living area that was furnished with period antiques, a long wooden table, chairs, a sideboard, and a buffet. Nautical paintings hung on the walls and huge windows looked out over the perfectly manicured lawn, shade trees, and flower gardens.

"I'll show you the kitchen." Leonard led the way to the back of the house where the kitchen stretched nearly the width of the home. French doors opened to the outside patio and high-end appliances, gleaming wood floors, polished countertops, and expensive cherrywood cabinets completed the chef's dream of a work space.

"Wow," was all Lin could say when she stepped into the room. A few moments later, she said as she ran her hand over the countertop of the kitchen island, "This is like something out of a magazine."

Wondering why Leonard had invited her and Nicky inside, Lin lifted her eyes to the man, but didn't know how to ask the question that was foremost in her mind so the two of them awkwardly staring at one another.

"Where's your lunchbox?" Lin looked around the kitchen for it.

"Maybe I forgot to make my lunch." Leonard gestured with his hand and stammered, "Why don't you wait in the living room and I'll hurry up and make my sandwich."

Lin looked at her friend with an odd expression, but gave a nod and headed into the room to wait. Everything was so pretty and perfect that she didn't want to sit, so she wandered around admiring the original paintings on the walls. A side table by the window held a collection of photographs in pewter frames set around a crystal flower vase. Lin leaned closer to look at them.

The pictures showed Leonard and his wife at their wedding, on the beach, riding bikes, painting the house, sitting together with friends on the back patio. The couple looked so happy and in love that tears formed in Lin's eyes.

A more formal photo of Marguerite showed the young woman to advantage with her shoulder-length, thick black hair, perfect skin, and deep blue eyes smiling out at the photographer. Lin's heart squeezed tight with sadness at what Leonard had lost.

At the corner of the table, next to another photo of Marguerite holding something in her hands, stood a sailor's valentine. There was a heart in the center of a compass rose all created with tiny pink, pale blue, and white shells which spread out in a pattern of small flowers to the edges of the box. The words, Remember Me, had been formed in an arc over the compass rose. In the photograph, Marguerite was holding the valentine close to her heart, her smile beaming at the person who was taking the picture.

Tears spilled from Lin's eyes and not wanting Leonard to come into the room and see her emotion, she quickly brushed at the drops of water on her cheeks and cleared her throat.

Suddenly, freezing air swirled around Lin making her shiver and she gripped the table to steady herself. Nicky whined. Lin slowly turned around.

Marguerite Reed stood next to the fireplace, her atoms sparkling and shimmering with a beautiful silver light, her blue eyes looking kindly in Lin's direction.

Lin gasped and stared at the apparition before her. The dog sat next to his owner, his little tail thumping on the floor and his gaze locked onto the spirit in front of him.

"Marguerite." The word slipped from Lin's lips as tears tumbled down her face.

The woman smiled sweetly at Lin and gave a slight nod before the particles of her body glowed golden and began swirling faster and faster until they sparked and disappeared.

Leonard stepped through the dining room into the living room carrying his lunchbox and when Lin saw him coming she batted at her cheeks and spun around so he wouldn't see her face.

"Coffin." Leonard's tone was tentative.

"Ready to go?" Lin asked without turning.

"What's wrong with you?"

"Nothing. Nothing at all. I got something in my eye."

"Did something scare you?"

Lin faced the man. "No. What do you mean?"

Leonard took some steps forward and scrutinized Lin's face and then he glanced down at the dog who let out a happy bark and tapped the floor with his tail.

"Did you get cold?" Leonard asked his friend.

Lin's eyebrows shot up her forehead. "What?"

"Did you get cold?" Leonard asked, his voice firm. "Did you see something?"

Lin lifted her eyes to her friend. Could Leonard see Marguerite? Did he think that *she* could see Marguerite? She forced an uneasy smile and asked in a joking voice, "What do you mean? Like a ghost or something?"

Leonard's face was serious. "That's exactly what I mean."

The tears began to fall again, but this time Lin didn't try to hide them. Instead, she hurried forward, wrapped Leonard in a hug, and pressed her face into her friend's chest.

24

Lin and Leonard sat together on the sofa talking.

"Oh, no." Lin suddenly remembered the new project meeting she and Leonard were supposed to be at.

"I postponed the meeting to tomorrow," Leonard informed Lin with a smile. "If things worked out here today, I knew we were going to have a lot to talk about."

With a smile, Lin nodded. "How did you know? How did you know I could see ghosts?"

"I didn't know for sure, but I wondered about it. Little things made me think so."

"You can see them, too." Lin's eyes danced with happiness.

"No, I can only see Marguerite."

Lin blinked. "Oh. Does she talk to you? Are you able to speak with each other?"

Leonard shook his head. "No. She sits with me in the evenings, she's in the kitchen when I make breakfast. I can usually tell what she's thinking by the way she looks at me. I talk to her all the time, but she isn't able to answer, or maybe I just can't hear her."

Lin explained that she could see spirits, but they never spoke to her. She told Leonard about the young boy who could see ghosts and hear them in his mind. "Sometimes I feel like I'm about to hear something, but it never happens."

"I thought you could see ghosts when we were at Liliana's funeral." Liliana was a close friend of Libby Hartnett and had very powerful paranormal gifts. "Marguerite was at the funeral. I figured other ghosts must be in attendance. I saw you watch as Marguerite walked up the hill. I wondered that day if you were like Liliana. And, you were at her house one day when she wasn't accepting visitors. I figured Liliana wanted to see you before she passed."

Leonard ran his hand through his hair. "Libby Hartnett and Liliana helped me when I lost Marguerite. In one of my drunken stupors, I let slip that I could see Marguerite's spirit. Libby talked to me a lot explaining that I wasn't crazy and she helped me better understand what was going on."

Lin sat straight. "Did Libby hint that I could see ghosts?"

"No way." Leonard shook his head. "She would never, ever do such a thing."

Lin realized that she should have known that Libby would never speak of her skills, but she let out a sigh of relief anyway. Remembering something, she looked at Leonard. "I saw Marguerite in town the other evening. I didn't know it was her at the time. She was watching me from across the street."

Leonard gave a nod. "I've been talking to Marguerite about having you come into the house. I wanted to be sure she was okay with it. If she wasn't, she wouldn't appear anyway, but I wanted to know she was okay if someone else knew she was here."

Lin touched Leonard's arm. "I'm so happy I don't have to hide this from you anymore."

"And I'm glad you know about Marguerite."

Lin glanced over to the table by the window. "You gave Marguerite a sailor's valentine?"

"Yeah, for her birthday."

Lin spent the next forty minutes telling Leonard about the old ghost, G. W. Weeks, the scallop shell piles, and the sailor's valentine she had recently purchased.

"You've got a lot on your plate, Coffin," Leonard said, causing Lin to chuckle.

"Too much sometimes," she told him.

Leonard got up to get the valentine he'd given to his wife and carried it over for Lin to see. "This one doesn't have any weird powers like the one you bought. It doesn't glow in the dark or show up in unexpected places."

Lin ran her hand over the glass cover of the valentine admiring the beautiful shellwork. "It's magnificent."

"It cost me an arm and a leg, but when we were in the store and I saw Marguerite's face when she saw the thing, I knew I had to get it for her." Leonard's face looked sad. "It was the last gift I ever gave her."

He coughed and cleared his throat. "See here." He pointed to the top at the back of the valentine. "Some valentines have a little slit to store a photograph or a note in. Sometimes the receiver of the valentine kept a photo of the loved one who gave her the gift in this little slot. Anyway, that's what the store owner told me when I bought it."

"Did Marguerite put a picture inside?" Lin asked.

"Yeah." Leonard used the tip of his finger to pull the photo out. It was a photograph of the couple on their wedding day.

Lin smiled when she saw the picture of Marguerite in her wedding dress and Leonard in a suit. "Oh, you both look wonderful."

"That was a long, long time ago." Leonard looked wistfully at the photo.

Something pinged in Lin's brain. As she jumped to her feet, she handed the photograph back to Leonard and said with excitement, "I think Marguerite's valentine just presented me with a clue."

Viv was standing in front of Lin's house when the truck came around the corner and pulled into the driveway.

"I just got here," Viv said. "Mallory's watching the store for me. What's up? What do you want me for?"

Unlocking the front door, Lin explained what happened when she went to pick up Leonard at his house. Viv stood in front of her cousin with her mouth open.

"He let you in?" Viv was thunderstruck. "You saw Marguerite?"

"It was Marguerite who was staring at me from the corner of the street in town the other night."

Viv's hand had flown to her throat. "I can't believe it. No wonder Leonard keeps people out of the house. Well, I suppose that isn't necessary since you're the only person I've ever met who could see a ghost, but it makes sense now. Leonard didn't want anyone sensing a ghost in his house. Wow. His wife stays with him? That's amazing." Viv looked at Lin. "But is it a good thing?"

"How do you mean?" Lin asked.

"You know." Viv glanced around the kitchen as if she thought a spirit might be lurking and listening. "Marguerite doesn't cross over. She stays here. Isn't that kind of like being in a state of limbo for her?"

Lin gave a helpless shrug. "I have no idea. Maybe she's waiting for Leonard to cross with her."

"Oh." The uncomfortable topic caused Viv to wring her hands together. "I didn't think of that." Her eyes narrowed in thought. "Does it make Leonard happy to have his wife's ghost in the house?"

"I think so." Lin led the way into the kitchen. "Wouldn't it?"

"I just wondered. He would never remarry with Marguerite still around, but having her ghost there might be hard. She can't converse with him. He can't go anywhere with her. He can't talk about her with other people. He can't kiss her or hug her or hold her. It makes me sad to think about it."

Lin put her keys to her truck on the island and frowned. "I didn't think of it that way. I don't know. Leonard seems happy."

"At least now you know why he was so odd about keeping you out of his house."

Lin gave a nod. "You should see the house. It's gorgeous inside, like something in an architectural or design magazine. Anyway," she looked over to the hutch to be sure the valentine was in its place, "Leonard gave Marguerite a sailor's valentine as a gift and he showed me that some of them have a little slit in the top to keep a photograph or a memento in it. Some people keep a picture of a loved one inside, others keep a note of love from a boyfriend or husband."

"You're going to see if there's a place to put an insert in the one you bought?" Viv asked.

"Yes." Lin looked warily at the valentine. "I wanted you to be with me." Shifting her eyes to her cousin, she said, "It scares me."

"What does? Finding something inside?"

Lin admitted, "The valentine scares me."

A worried expression washed over Viv's face. "Why? Why does it scare you?" She looked over at the object like it might fly through the air and strike her. "Did it do something to you?"

"No." Lin moved her hand around trying to dismiss her concerns. "It's just that it shows up in places, at the Whaling Museum, on top of the shell piles. It startles me. And sometimes, it glows. And remember how it was so hot when I first bought it that it felt like it might burn my skin?"

"I remember." Eyeing the object, Viv took a step back. "Do you think it will blow up or something if you look for a slit in the top?"

Lin looked at her cousin with horror. "Blow up?"

Viv said, "Maybe you should call Anton and have him look at it."

"I don't want to put Anton in any danger."

"Well, what about me?" Viv asked, her hand on her hip. "Are you putting me in danger?"

"You're supposed to be the one who calms me down, not makes me more frightened of the thing." Lin's cheeks had lost a bit of their healthy color.

Trying to keep her voice steady and encouraging, Viv put her hand on Lin's back and gave a little push.

"Go ahead. Nothing will happen. It's just a sailor's valentine. Go have a look."

Lin made eye contact with Viv, sucked in a deep breath, and knowing there really wasn't any choice, threw her shoulders back and strode with purpose over to the hutch. Lifting her hands to grasp the object, she hesitated for a moment, and then took hold of the valentine and removed it from the shelf. When she carried it to the kitchen island and set it down, Viv looked at it apprehensively.

"Don't make me nervous," Lin chided her cousin.

Lin ran her hands over the glass cover and around the wooden box.

"Is it hot?" Viv looked like she might dart from the room.

"No, its normal." Lin carefully moved her hands over the edges of the wood trying to find a place where a photo could be slipped in. "Nothing on this part." She turned the valentine to better see the other side, checked the edges, and then looked up at Viv with a wide smile. "There's a space here to slip something inside ... and there's something in it."

Lin used her finger to gently slide out a piece of paper. When it emerged from its hiding place, she unfolded the old, yellowed, slightly brittle paper. "A note."

Her eyes raced over the words and said to her cousin, "Viv. Come see this."

Lin read the words of the note out loud.

June 1836.

My name is George W. Weeks. I lost my beloved wife in childbirth two years ago. My infant son died with her. I have been distraught since that day. My dear friend, Robert Ward, came to visit me recently. We had drinks in the upstairs den. An argument ensued between us and we both said things we did not mean to utter. I threw the bottle of whiskey at Robert. In anger, he rushed away to the back staircase. I did not see what happened, but my dearest friend fell down the flight of stairs. When I reached him, he was at the bottom, dead. I did not know what to do. If I alerted the authorities, I was sure they would think I pushed Robert down the stairs intending to kill him.

In my panic and impaired state from too much drink, I put Robert's body in the wagon and drove in the darkness to the fishery lot by the harbor. I buried Robert there at the edge of the tree line. My dear friend. I am so sorry.

L IN LOOKED AT V IV. "It was an accident. Weeks didn't kill Robert Ward. He wants us to find him. He must want Ward to have a proper burial."

Viv reached out and touched the valentine. "That's why Weeks wanted you to buy the valentine, so you'd find the note and uncover the body. Weeks can't cross over because he hid his friend's body down by the harbor. Maybe Ward can't cross over until someone finds him."

"I'm going to call Anton," Lin said. "He'll need to help us explain all of this to the police."

When she crossed the kitchen to pick up her phone, movement on the deck caught Lin's eye and cold air whooshed around her.

G. W. Weeks stood outside holding his cane with his two hands. He stared at Lin through the window. They made eye contact for a few moments and then he nodded and tipped his tweed cap to the young woman.

A second later, his atoms glittered, broke apart, swirled in the air, and faded away.

25

I t took over ten days, but finally the remains of Robert Ward were located and uncovered by authorities. DNA tests were scheduled to be performed in order to match the man to his descendants, but the results would not be reported for weeks.

Lin was not in attendance when the man was found. She didn't know why, but she couldn't bring herself to stand by the scallop shell mounds and wait for Mr. Ward to be uncovered. Whenever Lin thought she should go see what was happening, terrible sadness washed over her and acted like a roadblock to keep her from heading to the site.

"It's okay," Viv told her. "You figured out the clues, put the puzzle together, and helped both

Weeks and Ward achieve a measure of peace. You don't need to be present while they dig. You need a break from all this. Anton is there. He'll report back to us."

Anton was at the shell lot by the harbor each day during the search for the body and did indeed keep them informed of the progress. "I have to admit my heart ached when the discovery was finally made. Poor Mr. Ward, lost and forgotten and alone for all of those years."

Lin's heart had also ached for George Weeks who, for nearly two hundred years, had carried the grief and regret of what he'd done in haste and from the fear of being accused of his friend's death.

"It's been set right now." Anton had patted Lin's hand. "Thanks to you and your skills."

A belated thirtieth birthday party for Lin and Viv was held at a restaurant down at the docks. A small, separate room with a private deck had been set aside for the family and friends to celebrate, and the festivities began with drinks and appetizers outside on the deck just as the sun was setting over Nantucket harbor. Swishes and streaks of violet and pink were painted over the blue sky and the air was warm and dry.

Viv and John, Lin and Jeff, Libby and Anton,

Leonard, and several other friends gathered to toast the three decades that each young woman had lived. Nicky and Queenie strolled around the deck amongst the people gathering pats and head rubs.

"Three decades?" Viv moaned. "Gosh. A third of my life is over."

"That's if you're lucky enough to live to be ninety," Anton told her. "Otherwise, you've already lived more than a third of your life."

Viv stared open-mouthed at the historian. "Oh, gosh."

"We're supposed to be celebrating our birthdays." Lin hugged her cousin. "Not bemoaning the passing of time."

"How can we avoid it?" Viv pouted. "Birthdays push it right in your face."

"Be proud of your age," Libby told Viv. "All we can do is live each day well."

"Thirty, though," Viv said. "It sounds so old."

Libby let out a laugh. "Wait until you're my age."

It was a beautiful evening, the dinner was served out on the deck, and the group chatted and laughed together for hours. Dessert was served as a buffet so that the guests could walk around the space, mingle, and enjoy several different kinds of sweets.

"You were away on the mainland for a long

time," Lin told Libby. "I kept wishing you were here. I felt lost during this case and didn't know what to do."

Libby's short silver blond hair glimmered under the lights. "Sometimes you just have to follow your ideas and intuition. If there's always someone around to look to for help, it prevents you from developing your skills."

Lin's eyes widened. "Wait. Were you here on-island all along?"

Libby avoided Lin's eyes and looked out over the harbor.

"You were here," Lin's voice was loud and a couple of guests looked over to see why she had shouted.

Anton approached the two women and when he saw the look on Lin's face, he started to back away.

"You told me Libby was on the mainland," she accused the historian.

"Don't blame me. I was only the messenger." Anton stammered. "Libby made me tell you that. She said it would help you hone your abilities if you thought you had to figure it out on your own. It was for your own good."

"Don't be annoyed with us, Carolin," Libby said gently. "Trust our experience in these matters." The older woman held Lin's eyes and then she looked pointedly around the deck at Jeff and Viv and then Anton. "And really, were you ever truly alone on the case?"

Jeff hurried over to the three people. "Some of Viv's and John's bandmates brought along their instruments. They're going to set up and play acoustically." He took Lin's hand and apologized to Libby and Anton for taking her away to dance.

Soon Jeff and Lin were joined by some of the other guests as they all danced under the stars. Nicky and Queenie had squished side-by-side together in a chair and watched the party-goers celebrate the two young women's birthdays.

"I'm glad that case is over and you can enjoy your birthday get-together," Jeff told Lin as they moved around the deck to the slow beat of a love song.

"Me, too. This one took a toll on me." Lin held tighter to her boyfriend. "I didn't understand that George Weeks was appearing from different time periods of his life to give me clues to what had happened. I still don't understand it."

"I guess you have to be open to unusual things that ghosts might throw at you." Jeff pushed a stray strand of Lin's hair out of her eyes and he smiled.

"Pretty soon, you'll be such an expert that there won't be anything that puzzles or surprises you."

"I don't think that day will ever come." Lin shook her head and then moved closer to Jeff. "Thank you for being here and helping and supporting me in this strange and crazy adventure."

Swaying to the music, Jeff held Lin's blue eyes with his own. "I wouldn't miss it for the world." He leaned down, touched her cheek, and kissed her.

Flickering lanterns had been placed here and there around the outdoor space and little, white twinkling lights wrapped around the deck railings sparkled against the darkness. The musicians had taken a break and the friends stood in groups of twos and threes, sipping drinks, eating slices of cake, and chatting together.

Leonard, dressed in off-white chinos, a light blue shirt, and a navy blazer, stood next to Lin watching the sailboats bob at their moorings. He shyly presented her with a pink gift bag.

"But we said no gifts," Lin smiled at the man.

"Well, I didn't spend any money, Coffin, so technically I followed the rules."

Lin unwrapped the tissue paper to see the sailor's valentine that Leonard had given to Marguerite on her last birthday. When she saw what it was, her eyes misted over and her throat tightened. "Leonard. But, it belonged to your wife. I can't...."

"Stop your blubbering, Coffin. I thought about it and now it's yours. It helped you solve your case. You helped two spirits find peace."

"But...."

"No, buts. Marguerite has no use for earthly objects. I have no need of things to remind me of her. You have a long life ahead of you. Pass it down to the daughter you'll have one day ... and when you do, tell her that only two things matter in life ... love and friendship."

Lin, choked with emotion, reached for Leonard's hand and pulled him into a hug as tears slipped over her eyelids and tumbled down her cheeks ... her heart full to bursting ... with those two most beautiful things.

I hope you enjoyed *The Haunted Valentine*! The next book in the series, *The Haunted Inn*, can be found here:

getbook.at/HauntedInn

THANK YOU FOR READING!

Books by J.A. WHITING can be found here:
www.amazon.com/author/jawhiting

To hear about new books and book sales, please sign
up for our mailing list at:
www.jawhiting.com

Your email will never be sold, shared, or spammed.

If you enjoyed the book, please consider leaving a
review. A few words are all that's needed. It would be
very much appreciated.

BOOKS BY J. A. WHITING

OLIVIA MILLER MYSTERIES (not cozy)

SWEET COVE PARANORMAL COZY MYSTERIES

LIN COFFIN PARANORMAL COZY MYSTERIES

CLAIRE ROLLINS COZY MYSTERIES

PAXTON PARK PARANORMAL COZY MYSTERIES

SEEING COLORS PARANORMAL COZY MYSTERIES

ELLA DANIELS WITCH COZY MYSTERIES

SWEET BEGINNINGS BOX SETS

SWEET ROMANCES by JENA WINTER

BOOKS BY J.A. WHITING & ARIEL SLICK

<u>GOOD HARBOR WITCHES PARANORMAL COZY
MYSTERIES</u>

BOOKS BY J.A. WHITING & AMANDA DIAMOND

PEACHTREE POINT COZY MYSTERIES

DIGGING UP SECRETS PARANORMAL COZY
MYSTERIES

.

BOOKS BY J.A. WHITING & MAY STENMARK

MAGICAL SLEUTH PARANORMAL WOMEN'S
FICTION COZY MYSTERIES

BOOKS BY J.A. WHITING & NELL MCCARTHY

HOPE HERRING PARANORMAL COZY MYSTERIES

TIPPERARY CARRIAGE COMPANY COZY
MYSTERIES

VISIT US

www.jawhiting.com

www.bookbub.com/authors/j-a-whiting

www.amazon.com/author/jawhiting

www.facebook.com/jawhitingauthor

www.bingebooks.com/author/ja-whiting

J. A. WHITING BOOKS

Printed in Great Britain
by Amazon